DEMCO

The Shuteyes

The Shuteyes

Mary James

JSF
JAME
c.l

**SCHOLASTIC
HARDCOVER**

Scholastic Inc.
New York

Library of Congress Cataloging-in-Publication Data

James, Mary, 1927–
    The shuteyes / by Mary James
        p.   cm.
    Summary: A boy is carried off by a giant one-eyed parrot to the planet
Alert, where sleeping is a crime and those caught in this activity are
contemptuously called "shuteyes."
    [1. Fantasy.   2. Prejudices — Fiction.]   I. Title.
PZ7.J15417Si   1993
[Fic] — c20   92-16170
                                                                  CIP
                                                                   AC

ISBN 0-590-45069-7

12 11 10 9 8 7 6 5 4 3 2 1   3   4   5   6   7   8/9

Printed in the U.S.A.   37

First Scholastic printing, February 1993

For Molly Allen

The Shuteyes

One night I saw an angry mob chasing these people who were still in their nightclothes. "Who are they after?" I asked, and the sneering answer came, "The shuteyes."

— from *Grabbing the Dream*, A Story of Abduction by Extraterrestrials

One

One day a huge, white, one-eyed parrot with a blue head flew into the kitchen window of my mother's restaurant.

"Am I here?" he asked my mother.

"Are you *where*?" she said.

"Here. Am I here?"

"You're in The Dream Cafe. Tell me your dream and I'll tell you the scheme against you."

"Are you *where*?" the parrot said.

"Don't say everything I say."

"Don't say everything I say."

"Chester?" my mother shouted, "Come in here! A talking bird has just arrived."

"Is he lost?" I asked. I never saw such a big bird, never saw one with a single eye the color of a lime and a long white feathery tail. "Can we keep him, Mom?"

My mother said what she always said when I wanted something and she didn't think I should have it.

"We can keep him the day something rhymes with orange."

Nothing rhymed with orange.

"I thought so," I said sadly.

"That day has come because we'll name him Lornge," my mother said.

"Lornge," said the bird.

"Wow!" I said.

"Lornge! Wow!" said the bird.

"He'll be good for business," said my mother. "I'm going to tell the customers this parrot has secret powers."

Two

"That bird never sleeps!" my mother complained. "You can cover his cage and he still talks! What kind of a parrot is he!"

"Alert," said the parrot.

"Oh, you're alert, all right!" my mother told him.

"Alert all right!" the parrot answered.

"Chester? You know who this bird reminds me of? Mr. Pye."

"The bird doesn't wear a white suit, and he doesn't eat M&M's, play Randy Travis and Waylon Jennings all day, and prowl through Old Muddy Swamp all night."

"No, but he's always awake!"

"Always awake!" said the parrot.

"Just like Gower Pye!"

My mother's name is Molly Dumbello.

The Dream Cafe was in the downstairs of our house.

Mr. Pye lived next door and he wasn't *always* awake because one day he told me he dreamed the same dream over and over.

"Tell my mother what your dream is and she'll tell you what schemes there are against you," I told him. "That's what my mother does: she interprets dreams."

The dream I dream over and over doesn't need interpreting," he said. "Its meaning is as plain as the nose on your face."

"What do you dream all the time?" I asked him.

"I dream that you and your mother are moving away."

"Is it my mother's drum that bothers you?" I asked him.

"Her drum is half the problem."

"And the other half?"

"Your questions, Chester Dumbello. Why this, why that, when will, how come, can a, does the, will it, won't he!"

My mother said she'd heard Mr. Pye went down to Old Muddy Swamp behind our houses nights, poled himself around in his flat-bottomed skiff, and caught cottonmouths to fry for his dinner.

"Snake eaters," she said, "are not a happy breed."

And to Lornge she said, "Is that why you don't ever sleep, Lornge? Are you afraid he'll start catching parrot for dinner some night while you're sleeping?"

Then Lornge said something he'd never heard from us.

"I'll get my zzzzzzz's if you please, I'll get my zzzzzzz's if you don't please."

"By all means, get them!" my mother said, and she said to me, "Where did that parrot learn that?"

Three

A week after my eleventh birthday, on the first day of summer, my mother's sister, Dolly, arrived.

My mother calls Aunt Dolly "Aunt Dollar" because she is so rich.

When Aunt Dolly came from Alabama to visit us in Mississippi, she arrived in a silver limousine that was as long as our front yard, with a chauffeur named Dearheart, who wore a black suit and a white cap and white gloves.

"Don't come in, Dearheart," she always called over her shoulder, "the customers in this place aren't used to chauffeurs. They'll stare at you."

He sat out front reading *Time* and *Life* and *Sports Illustrated*.

All the kids from the neighborhood came running down the block to see the Rolls Royce, and to tease me.

"Hey, Dumbell! Your aunt is a millionaire and your mother's crazy!" they'd shout.

I'd call back, "My aunt's a millionaire all right!"

"And your mother's crazy!" they'd persist.

I ran and they shouted after me, "If your aunt has so much money, why doesn't she buy a straightjacket for your mother?"

One day I told them all this lie, unaware that my mother was inside listening.

What I said was, "Dolly is my real mother. I'm just staying with Aunt Molly until she gets better."

The kids didn't believe me, anyway, but my mother said, "Whether they believe you or not, now they'll think that I embarrass you! *Me!* Your own mother!"

I said, "Well, it's not easy being your son. Do you have to beat that drum and sing so loud? Nobody else's mother beats a drum and sings!"

"Nobody else's mother has the gift of dream interpretation. I am gifted beyond belief and some-day you'll appreciate that, Chester Dumbello."

This summer day when Aunt Dolly arrived it was already getting dark, and there were no customers left in our cafe.

I could hear the kids outside calling out, "Your sister's here, Mrs. D! She's going to take you off to The Funny Farm!"

And, "Dumbell, where are you? Your chauffeur is waiting, Dumbell!"

"Molly," said my aunt to my mother, "I would like to take Chester back to Mobile with me, so he can have a taste of real life."

"You call your life *real*?" said my mother. "You call living in a house with forty-nine rooms *real*?"

"Forty-seven rooms. We don't count the kitchen or the pantry since only the servants go in there."

Aunt Dolly, my mother, and I were all blue-eyed blonds.

But Aunt Dolly was always in something silk with a big hat and heels so high birds could nest under them.

She was my mother's twin, married to a man who owned his own plane, had a diamond ring on every finger, and was nicknamed "Tux" because he always wore a tuxedo, day or night.

My mother was the kind of big woman whose dresses looked like tents. She wore a red and white bandanna on her head, and an enormous piece of crystal around her neck on a gold chain. Bracelets lined her arms, and she went barefoot even into the yard where there were pine nuts and evergreen needles that hurt my feet when I walked there without shoes.

In stores at the mall, in the movies, and on the streets of Lucy, the town where we lived, people turned smirking, to see my mother, not only because of her dress, but also because she was very loud and liable to say anything.

"So what? I'm different!" was her reaction when I cringed and sucked in my breath as we were noticed everywhere.

"You don't have to tell *me* that!" I answered her

in a bitter tone, and I thought of my dead father, who'd looked like a lot of other sailors since they all wore the same thing, and who'd done what the others did, since he was in the Navy and he had to.

My own secret plan was to join up myself as soon as I was old enough. Goodbye forever to being pointed out and stared at! When anyone asked me what I wanted to be when I grew up, I thought to myself: I want to be like everyone else, and I answered by saying, "A sailor."

My mother always said, "If you like marching in step, and coming home from war in a box, think about the Navy for a career," never dreaming that I did.

"Your father was a happy man, glad he had a son and a wife with a gift, so it's not a sad story. Too bad but not sad."

There was a picture of him in his sailor suit on her bureau. Across the bottom was written, *I'll sail home so keep a light burning for your husband, Chet.*

That's why we always had the front porch light on day and night.

"He can't come home if he's dead," I often complained, tired of being asked if we didn't know day from night over at our place.

My mother said, "Did he say keep a light on *unless* I'm dead?"

"But — "

"The light stays on until *I* die. Then you can turn it off and go live with your Aunt Dollar!"

That early evening at the beginning of summer, when my aunt was trying to talk my mother into taking me with her, and the kids were all outside yelling for me to show myself and be humiliated — here's what I heard from the kitchen.

"You're not getting Chester, Dolly!"

"Ask *him* why don't you?"

"Why should I?"

"So he can tell you himself he'd like to get away from the barefoot maniac and live with cultured people who have a piano and napkin rings and a swimming pool."

"Dolly," said my mother, "Chester doesn't care a fig for pianos and napkin rings and if he wants to swim in a pool he can walk over to Lucy Park."

Where they called me "dog doo from The Dream Cafe," ducked me, stole my trunks while I was in the water, and made me long to be anyone but me, anywhere but in Lucy, Mississippi.

"Molly," said my aunt, "call Chester in here and we'll see what he wants to do."

"Just because you're so rich, you think my boy will leave his own mother?"

"I'll make him his favorite Boston Cream Pie, and I'll get him his own dog, probably a big, friendly collie. I'll buy him the Suzuki GSXR-750 racing bike he dreams of owning, a pony named Sailor after his father, and Tux will take him up in our silver Aero Commander."

Aunt Dolly knew I could hear her.

Aunt Dolly knew the game show I was watching on television could not compete with mention of Boston Cream Pie, a big, friendly collie, a Suzuki GSXR-750 racing bike, a pony named Sailor after my father, and a silver Aero Commander.

I had to get out of there before I was asked if I wanted to spend the summer in Mississippi or Alabama. If I said Mississippi, lightning would strike me dead for lying, and if I said Alabama my mother's eyes would make me wish I was dead, the way they had when I lied to the neighborhood kids and said my aunt was my real mother.

I slipped on my baseball cap and headed out the back door even as Dolly began calling me.

It was almost dark by then and I ran through the back fields, toward Old Muddy Swamp, little brown bats above me tracing a pattern in the red sky.

Fireflies began dancing in front of me, frogs clunked, and owls hooted from the tupelo trees.

I was just about at Old Muddy when I heard Mr. Pye.

He was singing one of Waylon Jennings old songs, "What Bothers Me Most," in a voice filled with a twangy sadness, sounding like Willie Nelson, or Waylon himself.

The bottle-shaped cypress trees, some of them

as tall as sixty feet, had wide spreading tops and banners of Spanish moss draped over their limbs.

But dark as it was past twilight inside that swamp, I caught a glimpse of him in his white suit, poling his boat into shore.

I stopped in my tracks, a little edgy now about where I was, and what he might have caught, and what he could have done to me with no one there to see him, and me even more scared of snakes than being different.

There was a big, full, hot-looking moon hanging above.

When he stopped singing, there was silence except for the night noises and the lip of water kissing the muddy bank where I was standing, and he was heading.

I thought of dark, slippery lengths hidden in the swamp breaks, and I decided not to take another step forward.

I thought of calling out, "Mr. Pye? Is that you?" even though I knew who it was, if not for sure what he was up to. But I didn't trust him. It was one thing me hanging on his porch rail, calling questions into him, The Dream Cafe a few feet away and my mother right inside. It was another to be under this jungle roof with him, a man even more peculiar than Molly Dumbello on her worst days, a loner no one ever visited, said to have had some great tragedy befall him long before he ever settled in Lucy, and said, too, to live on snakes and the legs of frogs . . . and M&M's.

Green luna moths with thin long trailing tails on their wings, circled near my nose.

Then — what was it? A big sound. Suddenly a whole piece of the oozy muck in front of me heaved up, and a reptilian head with mad eyes and pointed fangs leapt forward.

I jumped. I slipped. I went into the swamp screaming bloody murder, and "Mr. Pyyyyyyyy-yyyyyye!"

Four

White teeth flashed in a grimace under the black mustache.

Strong arms inside the white suit wrapped around me. My jelly legs couldn't stand yet. My heart was hammering at my ribs, and I was turning deep sobs into a hoarse sounding cough.

"What was it?" I asked Mr. Pye. "A snake or an alligator."

"Just a lazy old croc seeing if you'd go good with what he had for supper." Mr. Pye let go of me then and said, "Stand up now. You can."

"Thanks," I said.

"Walk," he said. "You can."

I started to walk, dripping wet, teeth chattering in the muggy night.

He walked beside me. Tall with black hair. His white pants legs were rolled, wet and muddy now from pulling me out. So were his white high-top sneakers.

I wondered what I'd have done if he hadn't been

there. If he hadn't been there, would I have gone down to Old Muddy? I doubted it. For although he gave me the creeps — just the sight of him did — if he wasn't in Lucy then my own mother would be the major town crazy.

I liked watching him the same way neighborhood kids came down to stare at us.

He took out a few M&M's and popped them into his mouth, forgetting to offer me any, or maybe never intending to share them with me.

I wouldn't have minded having a couple. I hadn't had dinner yet. I said, "Do you ever eat anything besides M&M's, Mr. Pye," a little hint that was lost on him.

He said, "These things don't melt in my pocket."

"I guess Butterfingers would, and Milky Ways would, and Clark bars would, too."

"All of them would," he agreed.

"And you wear white all the time so you can't be too careful."

"No, you can't be."

We went along through the fireflies and the thousands of little mayflies my mother told me only live a day, don't eat, don't even have mouths, are born just to be food for bigger things. I wouldn't have minded not having a mouth myself that night because mine was watering hearing him suck on those things.

There were crickets singing and ducks and geese

squawking and honking from the rice fields. I knew
we were surrounded by things that creep and crawl
and lay in coils waiting for you.

Still shaken by my spill into the swamp, I said,
"How would you like to run into a rattler now?"

"You can smell them if they're around," said Mr.
Pye. "They smell like ripe watermelon."

He didn't say more. Mr. Pye never said much,
unless you asked him something. The longest thing
I ever remember him saying without being asked
was about the dream he had that my mother and
I would move away.

He didn't ask me what I was doing down by Old
Muddy after dark. He never asked me anything.

I didn't question him much anymore, either, ever
since he'd complained to me about it.

Nights I'd look over at his house, dark except
for the light from the television, or the little bulb
above his hi-fi if he was listening to his favorite
music. It was country since he said there was no
heart in other kinds, and heavy metal didn't have
a head or heart, in his opinion, which I'd asked, of
course, doing a headstand near his iron glider
where he'd sit with his straw hat on, smoking.

I'd wonder if he'd ever had or wished he had a
wife, or children. I'd wonder if it was possible that
I'd grow up and never marry, since who would
marry someone whose mother beat a drum in her
dirty feet and said a dream with a pig in it meant

there was a butcher knife hidden somewhere in your closet?

I got a spooky feeling us two walking along through the woods together, saying nothing, so I said, "Seen any good TV lately?"

"I only watch sports," said Mr. Pye.

"We watch sitcoms ourselves. You never do?"

"With that canned laughter?"

"I don't like it especially," I said. "Do you like game shows?"

"I said what I liked."

I guess I was just trying to keep him talking so I didn't hear the hoots and howls and squishes and whistles around me. And talking, he seemed more like other people.

There wasn't anything else to say, and I was already starting to worry about the bawling out I'd get when my mother saw me soaking wet.

We got to the field I'd run through behind our houses, and we crossed it, mosquitos nibbling at my legs and arms, and buzzing around my face.

When we got to our yards, I said, "Well, good night, and thanks again, Mr. Pye. You saved my life."

Whippoorwills were calling behind me in the black pines, and a mole was a heaving a run across the lawn.

Mr. Pye said, "Maybe there's nothing to thank

me for. How do you know you're going to have a
good life?"

"I don't," I said.

"Why don't you save your thanks until you're
sure," he said, and he turned left, to go to his place.

The next day he was gone.

He didn't take anything with him. His tube of
fresh mint gel Crest with the top off was on the
sink in his bathroom, toothbrush was there, razor.
His white socks and jockey shorts were in the
dresser with his shirts, and there was an unsmoked
Royal Casino cigar in a white plastic Arkansas Ra-
zorback ashtray on his dining room table.

The TV was going, and so was a window fan in
his front room.

No note, nothing.

We were all still talking about it way into August.

I was wondering if we drove him off but my
mother said when you run away you take your
underwear. When you disappear you don't.

Five

I liked summers best because there was no school and I did not have to face other kids.

The only one I ever hung out with was a girl called Rita Box-Bender, whose father home-schooled her. He sold angleworms, spot tail minnows, and dead flies, and a sign saying BAIT hung on a card table in front of their house. Underneath the table was a ball she'd made of tinfoil, too big to lift and good for nothing.

Kids called her Worms.

She was a little, white-faced redhead who'd be home learning to churn her own butter, and make soap from breakfast bacon grease and lye, while I'd be out at Lucy Middle School studying American History and English Composition.

One thing her father made her memorize was all these happy poems by a writer named Edgar Guest.

She'd come over to our house and recite them, and ask my mother if she could have a dream reading free in exchange.

One August morning this was the poem.

*It takes a heap o' livin' in a house t' make it
home,*
*A heap o' sun an' shadder, an' ye sometimes
have t' roam,*
*Afore ye really 'preciate the things ye lef'
behind,*
*An hunger fer 'em somehow, with 'em allus
on yer mind.*

"Did your father make you put that to memory,
Rita?" my mother asked her.

"Yes, Ma'am. I learned it yesterday."

"School's supposed to be out in the summer, isn't
it?"

"Home schools don't have regular vacations,
Mrs. D. Sometimes we take off right in the middle
of the week in the middle of March, and hunt down
red spider fern."

"Don't talk about spiders around me, please,"
my mother said. "I don't even interpret spider
dreams because they'll show up if you talk about
them."

"They will *not!*" I said . . . "will they?"

"They'll spin a web right over your bed, throw
down a line and crawl on your closed eyes. They're
not at all lucky, either. Some say they mean death
by choking."

"I was only talking about the fern, anyway, Mrs.
D., not a real red spider but I got a dream, if you'd

be kind enough to tell me its deep meaning."

She was way too little for a twelve-year-old, skinny like me, with this soft little voice that sounded like a whisper.

My mother said, "Put the mayonnaise away, clean off the cutting board, and give the crusts of bread to Lornge, and when everything's spic and span, I'll get out my drum. What did you dream?"

"I dreamed of a horse."

"Oh! Oh!" my mother said. "That's not good."

"Why?" said Worms.

"What is the lid on the mayonnaise jar doing in the sink? Look at all those crumbs on the floor? How can I give you an interpretation in a dirty kitchen?"

Worms got busy.

"Worms," said Lornge, even though we'd covered his cage to keep him quiet.

"Doesn't he ever sleep?" Worms said.

"Never does!" said my mother.

"What's good for insomnia is a tea of boneset leaves," said Worms. "My father taught me that in third grade."

"This bird's going to disappear like Mr. Pye did someday," said my mother, "only the reason will be a certain person could not take his day and night yapping. . . . Up there at that homeschool, do you have any recipes for baked parrot?"

Lornge said, "I tell no lies, nor shut my eyes."

"You mention sleep to that bird and he starts talking on his own," my mother said. "It's the strangest thing."

"Why does he do that?" Worms asked.

"How do I know? I have a lady out in the garden who dreamed her car was stolen," said my mother, "so now I have to get my drum and help her."

We could hear my mother out there under the weeping willow, as we swept the floor and put things away. I always helped Worms because she stuck up for me around the neighborhood kids, telling everyone my mother's dream interpretations were never wrong.

I think she missed her own mother, who died when Worms was a baby, and sometimes we wondered why we didn't get our two parents together so we'd both have a home and be brother and sister.

We talked about it that day, while my mother beat her drum outside and sang:

What do my dreams mean, Mrs. D?
Beat on your drum and tell me.
Leeches and spiders creep into my sleep,
So does my brother and nightworms who peep,
Tell me the meaning of bullfrogs with wings,
My dreams are filled with terrible things!

Worms said, "My father says he couldn't marry a woman who doesn't wear shoes."

"My mother doesn't like the sign in front of your house," I said.

"She beats that drum, too," said Worms.

"Your father's rumored to make moonshine, my mother's heard."

"I wouldn't mind her feet or her drum but he would."

"I wouldn't mind his sign or his moonshine but she would."

We were finding the whole idea impossible, as usual, when the lady in the garden with my mother began to cry. Loud.

"Are you *sure*, Mrs. D?"

"Yes. Someone wants to stop you from going to Texas to see your sister. Your dream is a warning. There's violence brewing."

"Violence?"

"Violent violence, yes, dear, I'm sorry. The drum is never wrong!"

Boo hoo. Boo hoo.

"The drum," I said to Worms, "may never be wrong, but it is never optimistic, either."

"Life is hard, that's why," said Worms.

"Mr. Pye once told me we don't know what our life is like yet. We have to wait and see before we say it's hard or happy. We have to save our opinion."

"We save everything up at our house. We save tinfoil, and we save paper, string, orange seeds, grapefruit rinds, and bureau drawer handles."

"Life is hard, that's why," said Lornge behind us.

The three of us were mulling all of this over when Mrs. Allentuck came running in from the garden to dry her eyes in the bathroom.

Outside under the weeping willow, my mother was tucking five dollars inside her blouse.

"Next!" she called out. "Rita?"

Six

"So you dreamed of a horse, Rita. Hmmmm. That means someone you know is going far away. Not you, or you'd be on the horse . . . but someone you know is going away . . . and now the drum is telling me more."

BOOM! BOOM! BOOM!

"Someone you know is going away,
Maybe today, maybe today,
Someone you'll miss is saying goodbye,
I don't know why, you don't know why.

"Someone you like is riding off soon,
Far as the moon, far as the moon,
You cannot go, you must stay here,
But be of good cheer, be of good cheer."

Lornge could hear them out there, too, and he whistled suddenly, something he'd never done before, and he called out, "Far as the moon, riding off soon!"

Seven

We had peanut butter and banana sandwiches for dinner that night with diet Dr Pepper.

"You made Worms very unhappy today," I said.

"It wasn't my fault she dreamed of a horse," said my mother.

"Why don't anyone's dreams have happy meanings?" I said.

"Chester, people don't come back to hear happy stuff. People like mystery. Even that poor little child needs some mystery in her life, or she'll end up talking to herself in the doorways of downtown stores someday. 'It takes a heap o' livin' in a house t' make it home' — is that how that doggerel went? There's no livin' up at her place with her old man turning her into a slave while he makes illegal whiskey out behind their barn."

"You don't know he does that."

"I know there's no money selling worms."

"So you just make up everything and say the drum tells it to you?"

"How can I explain it to you? I get a sense of

what is wrong in my customers' lives from what they dream. I intuit the rest."

"You what?"

"I intuit. I know something without reasoning it out."

"You guess," I said. "That's all you do."

"I'm a good guesser then."

"It's phony, Mom! People laugh at you."

"Let them. People don't have all the answers. For instance, where is Mr. Pye? No one knows, do they?"

"No one knows, do they?" Lornge said.

"Hush, Lornge. My son and I are having a private conversation."

"No one knows. Where is Mr. Pye?" Lornge said.

"That bird is going to drive me crazy!" my mother said.

"He's not going to have to drive you far," I said. "You're pretty close right now."

"That's disrespectful," said my mother.

I didn't say anything. I kept thinking of Worms running home in tears, and Mrs. Allentuck bawling her eyes out in our bathroom.

"Chester," my mother said, "I believe in a lot of things other people don't believe in. I believe there's no death, just another way to be, and I believe in other worlds and flying saucers and ghosts and angels and vampires and that sleep brings dreams that mean things."

Which started Lornge off again. "Sleepyhead go

to bed, have a dream, you're off beam."

"Whew!" said my mother. "I'd like to know where that bird came from!"

"Alert! Alert!"

"Alertetta, gentle Alertetta," my mother sang to the tune of "Alouette." "Alertetta, je te plumerai."

"This place is a loony bin," I said. "Get me out of here!"

The phone rang then. It was Mrs. Allentuck telling my mother her husband let the air out of the tires of her Buick, just as she was setting off for Houston.

"He was always jealous of my sister," she said, "and now he's going to pay!"

"Don't do anything rash," said my mother.

"Rash is not the word for what he's going to get when he walks through that front door!"

"See?" my mother said when she hung up. "I was right again! I definitely have a gift!"

"Don't do anything rash," said Lornge.

I got up from the table, shoving my chair back, heading out the front door. "Just get me out of here!" I said again to no one in particular . . . and least of all to Lornge.

Eight

I dreamed (I thought I dreamed) that I could fly, with Lornge beside me in the deep blue of the Delta's nighttime sky, filled with long lines of stars reaching down from the moon like great glistening fingers.

I never dreamed, and I wondered what my mother's drum would say this meant, when suddenly Lornge shouted over at me: "PULL YOUR LEGS UP FOR THE LANDING, CHESTER!"

My bottom slid along a surface soft as marshmallows with a puff of dust as we hit it.

I squealed, "What's happened to us Lornge?"

A thud.

I heard the distant sound of music, the *whump* of a bat hitting a ball, crowds cheering, and a voice calling "Hot dogs! Popcorn! Step right up!"

"Where are we, Lornge?"

"We're here, Chester. Now I can talk and be myself. Do you know how stupid I felt repeating everything anyone said to me over and over like a sleepy earth parrot?"

"Aren't we on earth now?"

"No, we're here now. We're on Alert."

Lornge was smiling and his big lime-colored eye had a new sparkle. He strutted in front of me proudly and said, "I got you out of there, Chester. That's what you wanted, right?"

"Did I?" I said, getting to my feet, my legs a little wobbly, my arms heavy at my sides.

"You said, 'Get me out of here!' Remember?"

"I say a lot of things."

"So do I, now that I'm back on Alert."

"Did I fly all by myself? Is that why my arms are tired?"

"Shhhhhh!" Lornge put a claw up to his beak and shook his head. "Don't say that word," he said.

"What word?"

Lornge whispered. "T-i-r-e-d . . . that's how I lost my mate. She couldn't help it, any more than you can. She was often t-i-r-e-d."

"From flying?"

"Sometimes from flying. Sometimes from nothing. She needed her — " Lornge looked around, his green eye watchful, and then he whispered again. "S-l-e-e-p," he said. "You see, Chester, she was not healthy. She refused to see a doctor. She said she liked s-l-e-e-p-i-n-g."

"What happened to her?" I asked him.

"They shot her down one night," he said, "even though it was off season to hunt, and even though

parrots aren't usually hunted. She simply refused
to fly twenty-four hours without resting." Lornge
flew up to my shoulder.

"But why would any bird want to fly twenty-four
hours without resting?"

"Because all birds here do, except sick birds,
and love birds. That's why I speak so well, because
of all the time I have to learn new words. No one
on Alert ever needs to rest, unless he's ill, in love,
or not normal."

"What does everyone do at night?"

"We play, of course. The night is to play in, unless
you're a baby. Babies play both day and night.
Listen!"

Whump! The sound of another bat hitting a ball,
more cheering, and a music from a band.

"That's everyone playing in The Stadium," said
Lornge.

I yawned, and Lornge covered my mouth with
his claw. "Shhhhhh! Don't make that noise."

"But I'm sleepy. I didn't get any sleep."

Lornge pecked at my ear. "Hush, Chester! We
don't talk like that on Alert. We don't say five letter words in polite company. We spell out those
words."

"What words do you mean?"

"S-l-e-e-p, t-i-r-e-d, w-e-a-r-y, s-n-o-r-e — those
kind of words . . . I promise you I'll find you a
secret place to nap."

"I'd just as soon go home," I said.

"You're going to your new home soon," said Lornge.

"No, I mean *home*. I mean The Dream Cafe. I mean the place where Molly Dumbello beats her drum in her dirty feet!"

"I can't believe you just said that, Chester. After all I've gone through for you."

"I didn't ask you to go through anything for me."

"Who were you begging to get you out of there?"

"That's just an expression, Lornge."

"You said it twice."

"I say it a lot."

"Well that's how you got out of there. . . . Now, Chester, soon you will go to your new home. No, don't wave your hands at me in protest. We are here now and it will be a while perhaps before we can leave here, for we don't travel to other places, that's the second thing we don't do."

"What's the first thing?"

"I thought I made that clear." He leaned down and whispered into my ear. "We don't s-l-e-e-p! Not ever! Never let your new parents know you s-l-e-e-p, do you promise? Never let anyone here know you need your zzzzz's. That's going to be our little secret."

Nine

"What a nice little boy!" said Mrs. Quick. "Quinten? Come in here and see our new son!"

She wore a white tennis dress and white tennis shoes. She had white hair worn in a long braid down her back, and held by a big blue ribbon. Her eyes were blue, too, and she smiled hard at me, then hugged me until it hurt.

Mr. Quick ran in from the yard carrying his golf club. He looked me over, never smiling once. His hair was red, like Worms' hair, and he was tall and skinny like her.

I had slept for five hours while Lornge guarded me, taking time off only to find shoes, trousers and a shirt for me since I had arrived on Alert in pajama bottoms only.

"Never admit you once owned pajamas," Lornge had warned me, "or that you even know what a bed is. There are no bedrooms here, naturally. There is no television, no slow music except for love songs which only lovers care about, and when we dance we whirl more. We do flings and things."

*   *   *

"Is this the best that dumb parrot could do?"
said Mr. Quick.

I said what Lornge had told me to say. "Thank
you for giving me a home, sir."

Mr. Quick was still shaking his head as though
he did not know what to make of me. "Mrs. Quick
and I always wanted a son," he said, "and neither
of us are getting any younger." He sighed and then
put out his hand for me to shake, saying, "I suppose
you'll have to do."

Lornge had warned me not to say much until I
got the hang of things on Alert.

"What kind of a handshake is that?" said Mr.
Quick. "I feel as though I just picked up a dead
fish."

"Sorry," I said.

"Our daughter is in college and we've been very
lonely," said Mrs. Quick.

"Because you're never home!" Mr. Quick said
sharply to her and to me he said, "Stand up
straight!"

"Quinten, don't pick on him so much!"

"He's my son now, isn't he?"

She said to me, "Our daughter's in college and
we've been very lonely, so welcome home."

"Thank you."

"Do you play golf?" said Mr. Quick.

"I never have."

"Never? What do you play?"

"Quinten, we said we would not ask questions. We have to get him some clothes."

"Tell me, my boy, are you a Brown or a Red?"

"What does that mean?" I asked, even though Lornge had said to try not to ask questions, or they would suspect me and I wouldn't have a home.

"Don't you even know if you're a Brown or a Red?" said Mr. Quick.

"No, I don't."

"Probably something ghastly happened to him before he got to us," said Mrs. Quick, who was plainly on my side. But Lornge had warned me not to be fooled by her kind manner, for she was the valued daughter of Ivan Investigate, Top Security Man, and in her own right was Top Scientist, working on a highly secret project.

"Even Quinneth Quick will not want to hear one word about your habit," Lornge had warned me. It was what he called the fact I needed sleep — my *habit* and he made it sound worse than dope or cigarette smoking or gambling.

"What is your name?" said Mr. Quick.

"Chester Dumbello."

"Chester Dumbello!" said Mrs. Quick. "What a melodious name."

Mr. Quick grimaced as he said "Dumbello. It's a little too melodious. Almost slack . . . like that handshake of his."

"There's nothing slack about this boy!" Mrs. Quick said. "But from now on you're Chester Quick. Are you hungry?"

"I wouldn't mind eating breakfast," I said.

"Breakfast, of course," said Mrs. Quick. "I'll get you some right now."

She left me standing there with Mr. Quick who was practicing swings with his golf club.

"Will Lornge be back?" I asked.

Mr. Quick seemed to sigh a lot. He sighed and said, "Yes, I'm afraid we're stuck with that old parrot. We told him he could live with us if he found us a son. He misses his mate, who was a beautiful blue-green, the color of our ocean."

"What ocean is that, sir?" I asked him.

He gave me a look. He said, "There's only one, Chester. The ocean is The Ocean. The sun is The Sun. The moon is The Moon. And the star is The Star."

"Yes, of course," I said.

"Naturally," he said. "As the old saying goes: one of everything is more than enough of anything."

"Naturally," I said.

"We have a daughter, and now we have a son," he said, "and also, it seems, an ignoramus of a parrot."

"Lornge," I said.

"What do you keep calling him?"

"Lornge," I said. "It rhymes with orange."

"Nothing rhymes with orange," he said.

He swung the golf club vigorously, as though he was mad at something. Probably at me, for not being what he wanted in a son.

He wasn't what I wanted in a father, either, for mine had sailed on all the oceans Mr. Quick did not seem to know existed. And mine had worn a uniform, and when mine walked down a street, any street, people called out, "Hello, sailor!"

"Parrots are trouble!" Mr. Quick announced, with another angry swing of his golf club. "They have the stick-by-me's. Every single one of them does. They get attached like scissors. They remain slowpokes all their lives, and if one of them happens to be like Tweetie was, that's the end of the other one."

He'd spat out the name "Tweetie."

He continued, "Parrots always bond hard, by nature. Why, if I was that attached to Mrs. Quick, how would I do my job and how would she do hers? How would I play my golf and how would she play her tennis? If we were a pair of silly parrots we'd be stuck together."

"Yes, sir."

"I told that parrot not to fall in love with Tweetie because we all knew what she was."

"Yes, sir."

"Tweetie was a beauty. I'll say that for her. And he fell madly in love with her. No one could tell him anything."

I jumped back, out of his way, as he hit an

imaginary ball with his club. He said, "Okay, you
fall in love. Okay, love slows us all down a little.
We all know that old tune. *But*," Mr. Quick's eyes
darkened and narrowed, "this Tweetie actually
used to s-l-e-e-p. Disgusting!"

"Disgusting!" I agreed, for I had learned in a very
short time that I did not think I would ever want
to disagree with Quinten Quick. I could "intuit"
that, as my mother would say.

And suddenly, the thought of my mother made
me homesick. And I wished I could look out the
window of The Dream Cafe, and see her under the
weeping willow tree, beating her drum. I wished I
could hear her singing: *Leeches and spiders creep
into my sleep/ So does my brother and nightworms who peep.* I would have given anything if
she would speak out in her deep voice: "A dream
with an iron in it means that soon you'll be crushed
by something, *or* you could have an excess of
phlegm in your bronchial passages!"

What would she think when she went into my
bedroom soon and found my empty bed?

"You look upset," said Mr. Quick. "What are you
thinking about, Chester?"

"I was thinking about what you just said, sir."

"Always think about what I just said and you
will make something of yourself yet, my son. Be
strong in this one life we have, and you will never
have to worry that they'll put *your* eye out, as they
did that parrot's!"

"Why did they do it to him, sir?"

"To remind him that we don't tolerate Tweetie's kind, pretty bird that she was, we *still* don't . . . and we certainly don't fall in love with one!"

"One *what?*, Mr. Quick."

He pursed his lips as though he'd tasted something sour, and said, "One shuteye, Chester! She was a shuteye! That's the worst thing you can be, and the worst name anyone can call you . . . but you know that."

Ten

At school next day, in Alertian History class, I studied The War Over Rhubarb won by The Browns one hundred years ago, up on The Mountain. There were many other wars for every year when the snow fell, they had War Week, The Browns and The Reds, fighting over everything from whose team had more warts to whose knew more songs backwards.

Alertian History was the only one taught, for though they seemed to acknowledge there was life somewhere beyond Alert, places they vaguely put under the heading Elsewhere, those living there were believed to be inferior and unwholesome, s-l-e-e-p-e-r-s, most of them. They wanted no contact with them, fearing the taint of the stranger.

In Careers class, I learned that most funeral directors lived in South Alert, and there, too, were manufactured all coffins, hospital couches, pillows, and all mats for exercise.

I listened as carefully as I could, to learn as much

as possible about my new home, which Lornge swore to me would be temporary.

He'd rubbed his blue head tenderly against mine, then looked straight at me with his big eye serious, and he'd promised, "There'll be a time to go back if you want to go back," adding, "But I doubt that you will when it comes."

"I *will*, Lornge. How could I ever be happy anywhere I have to hide when I sleep?"

Except for never needing sleep, most Alertians seemed little different from Mississippians, though down in the Delta we went at a slower pace. So did an Alertian named Cyril Speedway, for in our next to the last class of the day, he closed his eyes during The Dance of The Highway Signs, causing our dance teacher to tap him on the shoulder and say, "Cyr-rill? Cyr-RILL? What are you dooooo-ing?"

"What do you think he's doing?" said the girl behind me. "He's getting his ZZZZZZZZZ's!"

The class began to laugh uproariously, and Mrs. Fling charged back like a bull on the rampage, and jerked the girl to her feet.

"Do you want me to send you to the principal's office, Angel?"

"No. Please don't."

Cyril Speedway was bawling softly into his pocket handkerchief.

Only minutes before I had pretended my sweater

was making me hot, and as I pulled it over my head, I'd sneaked in a yawn.

"You know what your aunt will do to you if you're sent into the principal's office again?" Mrs. Fling was warning this girl.

"Please, please don't, Mrs. Fling."

The girl was a horsey sort with a whole mop of tightly screwed blonde curls, a place where flying things might easily hide. I thought she had a mean little mouth. You almost couldn't see her lips they were pressed together so tightly. One eyebrow was arched as though it would never come down until the day it saw something or someone equal to it.

"You didn't say you were sorry for speaking so obscenely, Angel!"

"I'm sorry."

"You'd better be. We're in a school of learning here, not in a filthy puddle where anything goes."

She started back up the aisle, and while her back was turned, the girl who'd just apologized whispered, "Cyril? Look!" Then she pressed her hands together and put them up to her cheek, dropped her head down on them, and closed her eyes. Closed her eyes just as Mrs. Fling turned back to the class, while everyone was snickering.

"ANG-GEL   WHEEL-SPINNER!   Get   out! NOW! Go to the principal's office! You are nothing but a bully."

"She has the nastiest mouth in this school!" said Cyril Speedway.

"Don't give her reason, then," Mrs. Fling told him.

Poetry was the last class of the day.

We spent it reading the collected works of Alert's Honor Poet, who seemed to enjoy remembering War Week through the years.

Just before the bell rang, our teacher, Mr. Lyric, gave us our next afternoon's assignment.

"Now the assignment is this/ the assignment is bliss. Reds compose a poem of home/ and Browns write of dad — aren't you glad?"

Then the bell sounded and everyone skipped off to play, while I remained at my desk, until Mr. Lyric noticed me there. He wore a baggy black suit, with a large red, floppy tie, no hair on his head, but a pencil mustache over his lip.

"Well, my fellow? Well, Dumbello?"

"Sir, I forgot that my name has been changed to Quick."

"That's not much of a trick. You are now Chester Quick."

"And, sir, I don't know if I'm a Brown or a Red?"

"Everyone knows their team, young Quick, but if you don't, then take a pick."

He curled his fingers into fists and held them out for me to choose.

I pointed to the left hand.

"Wherever you go, my lad, in this town, always remember that you are a Brown."

*   *   *

Lornge was waiting for me outside school.

"So am I a Brown," he told me. "Everyone is one thing or the other."

"Everyone?"

"Unless you live in The Sideshow, or at The Institute. Those who live there are too strange to be on any team."

"Why does everyone have to be on a team, though?"

"So you know which side you're on," said Lornge. "So you know who's on the same side during War Week."

"I don't want to be in a war, Lornge."

"We all go to war."

"My father was killed in a war."

"We don't kill each other here on Alert."

In front of us three boys and the girl named Angel had Cyril Speedway behind a bush. I could hear his cries as they punched him and pulled his hair. I could hear them call him the worst thing anyone on Alert could be called: "Shuteye"!

I said to Lornge, "Can't we help him?"

"Walk on by, Chester. I tried to help my wife and look what happened to me." He closed and opened his big eye for emphasis and shook his head sadly.

I hated listening to the sounds of Cyril crying out. Those sounds are the same anywhere, and I could remember when I would make them, hurt not just from the pummeling, but from not being liked, too.

I told Lornge about it as we walked along with him on my shoulder, headed for 3 Lake Lot, our new (temporary) home.

"But Cyril asks for it," said Lornge. "He does a lot of slack things like close his eyes to think, and stretch out down in the bushes by The Lake — I've seen him nights, staring up at The Star, with his hands behind his head. He's lazy more than anything else, but he comes off like a secret shuteye!"

"Like me."

"You can't help it any more than Tweetie could."

"Maybe he can't, either."

"Then he should be sent off to South Alert where most of them live. He should learn to be a mortician or a pillow maker. Shuteyes have a real talent for both things."

"I don't want to be a mortician, and I don't want to make pillows!"

Lornge nudged my neck with his beak. "You're different, pal."

"I'm *glad* I am! I never heard of people who don't sleep!"

"We haven't heard of you, either. Oh, I have. I *had* to learn about you, but here we aren't interested in anything that's Elsewhere."

"What I don't understand," I said, "is where is this place? Are we on another planet?"

"I can't discuss it with an outsider, Chester. We

vow never to, should an outsider come here, which nobody expects will happen in a million years!"

"But don't these people want contact with other civilizations?"

"Yes, if there were any others, we would."

"What about earth?"

"A mess. Earth is a mess. Earth scares me. The whole time I was there, I was terrified. I thought a war would break out, a bomb would go off, something horrible!"

I said, "Mr. Lyric said wherever I go in this town, to always remember I'm a Brown."

"You won't forget that, will you, Chester?"

"But what town are we in?"

"We're in Alert."

"I thought at least it was a country, maybe even a star."

"It's whatever you want to call it," said Lornge. "Mr. Lyric always has to rhyme what he says, and Brown rhymes with town."

"But Lornge," I protested, feeling tired and therefore crabby, "I don't — I — ewwww, ahhh!" I yawned right in the middle of what I was going to say next.

"You need a nap," said Lornge. "We'll do something about it immediately, but be quiet. And thank The lucky Star you're not popular here, either, for if anyone had chosen to walk home with you, and seen you do what you just did, you'd be called names and picked on, at best."

"What about at worst?"

"Sent down to South Alert to live, unless of course they catch you in the act. You can go to The Tower of Loathing for s-l-e-e-p-i-n-g." Lornge hopped around on my shoulder looking all around him, making sure it was safe to talk about it.

"But don't worry," Lornge said, nudging me affectionately with his beak, "I'm not going to let anything happen to *you*!"

Eleven

The crescent Moon and The single glittering Star were overhead as I looked up from the bottom of the Sports Equipment Shed.

It was at the end of The Quicks' property. The lid was pushed back, and Lornge was perched on it, guarding over me.

"Awake?" he whispered.

"Why are you whispering? No one's around, is there?"

"Your new father is off playing golf, and your new mother is down playing tennis, but the neighbors might be next door."

"I don't mind so much having a new father," I said, "but my real mother is still alive, so please don't call Mrs. Quick my new mother — not when we're alone, Lornge."

"You don't miss her, do you?"

"Of course I miss her!"

"It's not fair to me to miss her. I rescued you, after all. I got you out of there."

"But I don't like being a secret shuteye, and I

miss The Marshmallow Dream Cakes that my mother made. I don't write poems well, either, and now I have to write one for homework. In Mississippi we never had to write a dumb poem!"

"You said get me out of there and I got you out of there! You were not happy there! Once you even said your aunt was your real mother, remember? You were so embarrassed by the drum, and the song, and the very bad things she said dreams meant."

"Don't remind me of my happy past."

"When your mother said that I was driving her crazy, you even said she wouldn't have to drive far."

"That was before I really knew what she said came true. She could intuit better than anyone! She said you had secret powers, and you do or I wouldn't be here. She told Worms someone she knew was going away soon, far as the moon."

"Far as the moon," Lornge agreed.

"And that someone was me."

That was the moment we heard all the noise from next door, and it was the moment, too, when I saw my first Star Reacher.

"Do you call this a poem about home?" a woman was screeching. "Harold? Listen to this poem about home your daughter wrote!"

Then she began, and we could have heard her even if we'd left the yard, gone into the house, and shut the door.

But we didn't. I couldn't. I couldn't tear my eyes from the great silver structure in the same yard where the woman was shrieking.

"H — a hat, a hat I hate,
A — an address on Lake Lot
T — the trap that is my life
E — the energy she's got!
H — the horror of my life,
O — the onus and the strife
M — the misery I feel
E — the edge toward which I reel.

Put them all together they spell Hate Home,
Which is the title of this new poem!

"What a brilliant poem!" said Lornge. "She *is* trapped, too. Her aunt is always forcing her to do things."

"I wouldn't mind being trapped in a yard with something like that in it. What is it, Lornge?"

"It's a slide. It's called a Star Reacher."

"I've never seen a slide that tall. In Mississippi our downtown buildings aren't that high."

"You go up to the top in a chair lift, and then you zoom down into a pool. . . . Her father manufactures them."

"She must be a Red, since Reds had to write a poem about home."

"That's Angel Wheelspinner."

"The mean-mouthed bully from school?"

"Yes," said Lornge. "She's from the richest family in Alert. I hate that aunt of hers, too, since she wears a hat made of parrot feathers. I think some of my poor, precious Tweetie might be up there on her head. They sold her feathers she was so beautiful."

We could not hear what Mr. Wheelspinner had to say about his daughter's poem. We only heard him mumbling.

"Angel!" Maud Wheelspinner screeched again. "Come out here on the patio! You are to write a new poem immediately, and if you do not, you will come to The Sideshow with me tomorrow and sit there until you do!"

We were putting the top back on the Sports Equipment Shed, and shaking out the first base bag I'd used as a pillow.

We could hear Angel Wheelspinner whining back that she could not write a better poem about home.

"Then you'll come to The Sideshow with me!" her aunt yelled.

As Lornge and I headed up the yard, I said, "And I thought my aunt was bad."

"Yours is. She's selfish and self-centered."

"Aunt Dolly," I said fondly. "I could have been in Mobile with her right now, using napkin rings, playing the piano, going up in the silver Aero Commander."

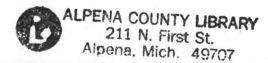

"You must put Mississippi out of your mind," said Lornge.

"Mobile's in Alabama," I said.

"Put all of that out of your mind, for now. You are my best friend now. We are a pair. We are like scissors."

"We're not enough alike to be scissors," I said.

"We can still think of ourselves that way."

"What is The Sideshow?" I asked Lornge, "And why is Angel's aunt going to take her there if she doesn't write a new poem?"

"Maud Wheelspinner is Top Curator of The Sideshow," said Lornge.

"Is The Sideshow open nights, Lornge?"

"I don't know."

"Is it far from here?"

"It's neither near nor far."

"Can we go there, Lornge?"

"Don't *you* have a poem to write, too?" Lornge changed the subject.

Twelve

"I'm told The Browns at school were assigned a poem about their dads," said Mr. Quick, changing from his golf gear into his swimsuit. "If you recite yours for me, I'll take you next door for a ride on The Star Reacher."

"That's just what I was hoping for!"

"Well, then?" Mr. Quick handed me a new brown bathing suit and said, "Brown for a Brown," and snapping the elastic on his own, he added, "And Red for a Red . . . let's hear your poem."

I was not good at writing poems, but I had been working on mine ever since my nap, and my glimpse of The Star Reacher.

I recited it as I got out of my clothes.

> *"If my dad, Mr. Quick,*
> *Told me I could take my pick,*
> *Of anyplace I'd like to go,*
> *I'd say next door,*
> *Please, let us ride,*
> *Down that slide."*

"Chester," said Mr. Quick, "your rhyme is slightly off. Go doesn't rhyme with door."

"I have a Southern accent," I said. "Door sounds like doe."

"What is this about a Southern accent, Chester? Nobody in South Alert *sounds* any different. They just behave differently, and vilely! Were you being a smartass? What do you know about South Alert?"

"Nothing," I said, remembering that their South did not mean my dear old Dixie.

"Are you curious about South Alert?" he barked at me.

"No, sir." I said.

"There's plenty of time to find out about Lullaby Land," he snickered.

"Plenty of time," I snickered back, though I have never been good at snickering, poetry writing or speaking out.

I gave speaking out a try. "I'd really like to go on The Star Reacher."

"Let's change the poem then. Let's say: *If Mr. Quick, my dad, asked me/ where would you be glad to be?/ Next door, I'd say/ on that great ride/ Down that slide, down that slide.*" Mr. Quick looked very pleased with himself.

He said, "That's better, isn't it?"

"That's much better," I said.

I put on my new brown trunks. He passed me a piece of Pep-Up Peppermint Gum. Off we went toward the Wheelspinners.

The Star was shining bright in the sky and The crescent Moon was next to it.

"Mr. Quick? How did the Wheelspinners get so rich if not many people can afford Star Reachers?"

"Maud Wheelspinner has all the money in that house," he told me. "She wouldn't have to work if she didn't want to, but she loves to hunt down freaks for that Sideshow of hers."

Thirteen

"How is business?" Mr. Quick asked Mr. Wheelspinner.

"I almost sold a Star Reacher just yesterday morning," he answered as he waddled closer, a fat man with yellow curls like his daughter's. "How is your business, Quinten?"

"I sold six bathtubs and five toilets," said Mr. Quick who owned the Bathe and Flush shop.

"And Quinneth? How is her work at The Institute?"

This was the first I'd heard she worked there, whatever it was, whatever went on there. Lornge said they studied mysterious things there and did not welcome visitors.

"Quinneth is doing top secret work, as usual," Mr. Quick said. "Busy, busy, busy, as usual. And Maud? How is her work?"

I wished they would get their conversation over so we could go on the slide. The chair lift was heading toward the top and I could see the backs of two heads: a blond one and a gray one.

"My sister is busy as ever," said Mr. Wheel-spinner.

"I hear there's a new freak at The Sideshow."

"Another male, yes."

"Next rainy night I'll take you there, Chester." Mr. Quick rarely called me "son." He seemed to have trouble saying the word, just as I could only think of him as *Mr.*

"Is it far from here?" I asked him.

"Not far at all. It's at the end of Lake Lot."

"It *is*?" I said. I wondered why Lornge had not told me that when I first asked him about it.

"It's right down on The Lake," said Mr. Wheel-spinner. You can see it from the top of The Star Reacher."

At the mention of the slide, we three glanced up in time to see Maud Wheelspinner pushing her niece toward the slide, while Angel held fast to the bar on the chair lift, squealing, "Stop! Stop!"

"My daughter has a fear of heights," said Mr. Wheelspinner. "My sister's probably getting her over it."

"It doesn't look that way to me," I said.

"It looks the way Mr. Wheelspinner says it looks," said Mr. Quick, and he gave me a nudge.

Maud Wheelspinner's voice carried in the evening wind. "Now, you little brat — is E for the edge toward which you reel, or is E for Excuse Me for writing such a hateful poem?"

"E is for the edge toward which I reel!"

Mrs. Wheelspinner reached out and shook her.

"She's shaking her," I said. "That was a very hard shake."

"It is very hard to get over a fear of heights," said Mr. Wheelspinner.

"Very hard to get over a fear of heights," Mr. Quick agreed.

"It's that poem she's trying to get her over, if you ask me," I said.

"Which nobody did," said Mr. Quick.

"Which nobody will," said Mr. Wheelspinner.

Then Maud Wheelspinner began again, pushing her toward the slide, shouting at her, "Are you going to write a nicer poem about home or would you rather take a little ride?"

"No, please!" Angel's voice had lost its sharp edge, and something sank inside me. For even though she was a nasty-mouthed bully, I felt pity for her. I had had my own bad moments being ducked under the water at Lucy Park, swallowing chlorine and deciding to agree that my mother was so psycho she should be put in a cage and labeled NUT CASE!, if I could only get another gasp of air and have the opportunity to say it.

I could not see Maud Wheelspinner's face. They looked like stick figures way up there, but we could hear them clearly.

"Are you going to write a nicer poem about home?"

"I'll try, Auntie."

"Didn't you hear me, Brat? I asked you are you going to write a nicer poem about home?"

"Boo hoo. Yes, Auntie, I'll really try!"

"Trying isn't good enough. I don't like efforts. I like solid results! Do you understand me?"

I could see the stick figure which was Mrs. Wheelspinnner leaning menacingly toward Angel again, shaking her finger at her.

Angel was leaning back, hanging to the rail of The Star Reacher and bawling.

"Do you want to go for a ride, Dear? Wouldn't a ride be just the thing to inspire you to write another poem?"

"I don't want a ride, no, I *don't!*"

Mr. Wheelspinner had toddled back inside the house while all of that was going on. Mr. Quick was doing handstands down the lawn, extolling the joys of tumbling.

"If my customers tumbled more, they'd flush more," he said.

Now the chair lift was starting down to pick up Mr. Quick and me.

"And exercise keeps the Southies away, too," he said.

I had to keep reminding myself that "South" meant South Alert, that "Southie" was the Alertian

slang for funeral director, and "go to s-l-e-e-p"
meant Drop Dead there.

Soon the night was filled with the terrified
screaming of Angel Wheelspinner as she barreled
down the slide and into the water.

Fourteen

In all my life I had never been on such a thrilling ride, swooshing through the twists and turns recklessly, like the front car of a roller coaster, roaring down in the darkness, flying through the air at the end, then SPLASHDOWN!

Mr. Quick was talking with Maud Wheelspinner back on the top of the slide.

I was swimming toward the pool ladder with a pounding heart, but grinning in the cool night air at the excitement, wanting to catch the lift again, go right back up, come right back down.

Sitting there, dangling her feet in the water, a notebook on her lap, a pencil in her hand, Angel Wheelspinner looked haggard from her ride of terror.

She said, "What rhymes with home beside poem?"

"Roam," I said, pulling myself out of the pool, jumping on one leg, punching my head to let the water out of my ear.

"Comb, too . . . I'd like to comb her from my home."

"Don't keep thinking that way," I said. "She'll only get even with you."

"I know it. If you tell anybody at school what you just saw, I'll say you're a shuteye! I *will!*"

"You don't have to threaten me," I told her. "I wouldn't tell on you."

"Everyone thinks it's so wonderful to be living with the Top Curator of The Sideshow!"

"I hope she doesn't treat the animals that way."

"They don't have that many animals. Now that the parrot is living with you, they don't even have a bird."

"Was Lornge living in The Sideshow?"

"He was there about a year."

"Lornge?"

"There's only one one-eyed parrot on Alert. You can call him whatever you want."

"Why was he in The Sideshow?"

"He was in there for loving a shuteye. He loved a shuteye. He even mated with one. He even called one his wife."

"Why isn't he still there then?"

"Ask him," she shrugged. "I don't have any interest in shuteye birds or shuteye people!"

"Why do you pick on Cyril Speedway?"

"Speaking of shuteyes," she said snidely. "He may really be one, you know. I suspect he s-l-e-e-p-s in secret."

"What if he does?"

"What if he *does*?" She shot me a look of amazement, as though she could not believe what I'd said.

"What do you care," I asked her.

"What do I *care*?"

"Yes," I said. "Why does it bother you?"

"My father says if you hang around with ducks, soon you start to waddle, and if you hang around with cows, soon you start to moo."

"You think if you hang around with Cyril you'll close your eyes or something like that?"

"Yes. Close my eyes, and maybe even yawn."

Yawn.

Why did she have to say that word.

Who can hear the word "yawn," and not yawn?

In Alert the word "yawn" didn't make people yawn, but I was forced to turn away from Angel, and pretend to look for Mr. Quick at the top of The Star Reacher. I yawnnnnned, quietly as I could, sure she might even hear my jaws move it was such a long, luxurious yawn.

"Did you write your poem about your dad?" she asked me.

"Yes," I said.

"Mr. Quick doesn't seem like your dad. And Mrs. Quick is too busy to be anybody's mother. She does secret experiments, I hear." She kicked the water with her feet. "I wish The Reds could write a poem about their house instead of their home. More

things rhyme with house. Louse, for instance. The
louse in my house."

"Try not to think so negatively," I said.

"Spouse, mouse, souse," she said. "Oh, I'm never
going to get a poem written before the night is
over — never! She's going to kill me!"

I could not believe that I was seeing tears in the
very eyes that seemed so vicious just that afternoon.

"Wait a minute!" I said. "You just made me think
of something . . . House . . . Home . . . House . . .
Home . . . something is coming to me."

"Is it a poem, Chester?"

"It is."

It was not my poem, of course, but that one of
Edgar Guest's which Worms had recited in The
Dream Cafe. And in exchange for her recitation,
my mother'd interpreted her dream for her. A
dream of a horse.

> *Someone you like is riding off soon,*
> *Far as the moon, far as the moon.*

I would never forget it.

"Start writing!" I said.

She pointed her pencil at her notebook and said,
"Ready and set to go."

I dictated from memory, beginning:

*It takes a heap o' livin' in a house t' make it
home,*

A heap o' sun an' shadder, an' ye sometimes have t' roam . . .

When she had finished taking it all down, she looked up at me and said, "I won't forget this, Dumbello."

I did not bother to correct her, for I missed hearing my old name.

"I hope I've solved your problem."

"You have. You have. Except I'm going to make a change or two. I'm going to write: *It takes a heap of living in a house to make it home.* See what I mean?"

"Yes. You're changing heap 'o to heap of, and t' to to."

"I am," said Angel. "The poem is just what I need except you seem to have a bad case of the cutes."

Fifteen

"The reason there were no movies or television on Alert," Lornge said, "was that it encouraged needless reclining."

"Think about it," he said. "You start watching it and next your slumped down in a chair watching it, and next you could feel w-o-o-z-y."

"Don't you people ever just give in and rest?"

"I told you, Chester, we don't need rest. But anyone can get into lazy habits, so we don't have movies or thank The Star, TV. I used to hate living in The Dream Cafe at night because of all the sitcoms your mother liked."

"Don't remind me," I said sadly. "I would give anything to hear the sound of canned laughter again, of CBS nightly news, of the weathermen who say it will be sunny when it turns out to be rainy, and say it will be rainy when it turns out to be sunny. I would give anything to hear the squeals of happiness from someone winning a houseboat equipped with Formica kitchen counters on a game show, or to just know who's at war."

"You should have forgotten about all that long ago," said Lornge. "You're not adjusting well."

This was one of our nightly conversations just after I awakened in the Sports Equipment Shed.

Usually I was in my best mood then, for I would manage five or six hours sleep while Mrs. Quick was still at The Institute, and Mr. Quick played backgammon with Angel's father, before late dinner.

Mr. Quick believed I was at a youngster's Play-Park.

This night I was not in such a good mood, despite my sleep. And perhaps because my sleep had been interrupted by a loud humming sound.

I called up to Lornge, "What *is* that?"

"It's The S-l-e-e-p-y People Choir from South Alert," he called down to me. "They hum to announce their protest marches and their s-l-e-e-p-i-n-s. Right behind them is The Nightdress Brigade parading in support."

I lay there listening, for I was very tired from the long day and the constant process of learning all about Alert.

At first it sounded so like something from home and long ago, that tears welled up in my eyes.

It sounded like Christmas, like church, like our local barbershop quartet The Delta Stars, warming up to entertain at summer fairs, ready to burst into "Oh, Susannah" or "Tie a Yellow Ribbon 'Round the Old Oak Tree."

Then in eerie, slow, and sad high-pitched tones
I heard them croon:

> *Lull a, lool a, lulla by*
> *Lull a, lool a, lulla by.*
> *Lull a   by*
> *Loll a   by*
> *Lull a*
> *Loll a,*
> *Lull a*
> *Byeeeeeeeeeeeeeeeee*
> *Sleep! Sleep! Sleep!*

Sleepy as I was myself, I wanted to see them,
and I was just pulling myself up to peer out the
top of the shed.

Then it happened.

A long line of motorcycles descended on the
column of choristers, running into them, snarling
at them *"Shuteyes!,"* konking them over their
heads with their billy clubs, laughing and not
bothering to spell out the S word: "Go to sleep,
Shuteyes!"

"What happens to them now?" I asked Lornge.

"They'll go back to South Alert, those who don't
end up in The Hospital."

"They call South Alert 'Lullaby Land,' too, right?"

"Shhhh, Chester. That's not nice to say."

"But they were singing a lullaby and it was so
sweet!"

"There is no such thing as a sweet lullaby. Lullaby is automatically not nice, the way certain four letter words you can think of are not nice where you live."

"Don't you like lullabies, Lornge?"

"Of course I don't like them! They're slack! Even though they remind me of Tweetie, truth be known they disgust me. Why sing about something as sick as s-l-e-e-p? If you must s-l-e-e-p, find someplace where no one will see you do it."

"Like a Sports Equipment Shed," I said bitterly.

"Yes, as a matter of fact," said Lornge. "After all, you don't go to the bathroom in front of people. And s-l-e-e-p is something like that, isn't it? You relieve yourself, don't you? You relieve yourself in private, if you have that problem, and you don't march around singing about it, do you?"

"It's not at all like going to the bathroom," I said.

"Isn't it a relief?"

"Yes, but — "

Lornge put his claw up to his beak. "Hush! We've had quite enough bedroom talk."

"You don't even have bedrooms here!" I said angrily.

"There are bedrooms in Lullaby Land," said Lorgne, "and some of the shuteyes boast about how soft their beds are. Ukkkkkk! We must stop this talk. It makes me feel like puking."

"Then I must make you feel that way, too."

"I've bonded with you now, Chester, and I can

never turn against you. But even when I was hanging out with Tweetie's crowd, I felt what they did was wrong . . . besides, *you* can't help it, coming from earth. It's natural to you."

"I love sleep! I hate it that you don't!"

"Shhhhh! Chester. Chester. It's bad enough what you are. Don't brag about it."

That very night on the Alert Public Radio, which was on the air only twice a day, for morning and evening news, we heard about the shuteye march up to Lake Lot.

Why anyone would wish to proclaim pride in s-l-e-e-p is beyond understanding, but the shut-eyes were out marching again today, going into the respectable neighborhood of Lot Lake. Little children looked on bewildered by these sickos with the Radical S-l-e-e-p-e-r-s accompanying The S-l-e-e-p-y People Choir, wearing signboards saying (and I am not making this up):

We'll get our zzzzzz's if we please!

'Night is might!
S-l-e-e-p is right!

Don't s-l-e-e-p in secret!
S-l-e-e-p in bedrooms!

How fitting that these shuteyes come into our neighborhoods humming, warning us of their evil in animalistic style: as bees warn us, as rattlesnakes give warning.

At least the freaks from The Sideshow have an excuse for their bad habits, since Elsewhere has never evolved properly, but what excuse is there for shuteyes? They are a blight on Alert!

I vote to cast them out, all of them!

This is your Alert newscaster wishing you a good good evening of play and games!

Mr. Quick had come into the house as the news was ending, and he sat down across from me while an announcer said, "*A final note: Alert's Poetry Teacher, Lawrence Lyric, announced today that this semester's school contest was won by a Red.*

Her name is Angel Wheelspinner of Lake Lot, and here is Mr. Lyric to read you a little masterpiece called simply "Home.""

Mr. Lyric began, " 'It takes a heap of living in a house to make it home, A heap of — ' "

"Good evening, sir," I said.

"Shhhhh! I want to hear this," said Mr. Quick.

At school assembly that morning, Angel had found a seat behind Cyril Speedway. When the principal got up to make his morning report, Angel made deep snoring noises as she leaned very close to Cyril.

When the principal asked who dared to s-n-o-r-e, Angel pointed at Cyril, who was sent home with a warning note.

Angel was the school clown. Whenever I saw her face in the halls, the classes, and on the running fields, it was always lit up with the joy of doing something mean. This made the other kids want her around.

"What will Angel do next!" kids often said.

And Angel's answer was always, "Something more terrible than what I last did. You'll see!" And she'd let go this wild giggle that lasted several seconds and ended in a snort, but not a snore.

When the poem was finished, Mr. Quick said, "Her poem about home praised her home, but your poem about me wasn't really about me, was it?"

"You changed it yourself, sir."

"I changed it but I didn't really understand the assignment. You really wrote a poem about wanting a ride on The Star Reacher. Angel stuck to the assignment but you did not. You don't follow orders."

"I helped Angel with her poem," I said.

"So I hear, but maybe you should have concentrated more on your own poem. Maybe you should have written something like: *Of all the dads that I could pick,/ no better is there than Q. Quick.*"

"Yes, sir," I said.

"Of course if you hadn't helped Angel, you

wouldn't be going where you're going this evening."

"Where's that?"

"We've been invited by Maud Wheelspinner to be her guest at The Sideshow. It's her way of thanking you for helping Angel bring the public's attention to her happy home. Angel's aunt thinks you're a good influence."

"Maybe I am," I shrugged. "When do we start off for The Sideshow?"

Lornge flew from my shoulder to his cage, as he always did when he wanted no part of something.

"After we have dinner," Mr. Quick said. "And Chester?"

"What?"

"Next time don't let a girl beat you."

Sixteen

"Someday *you'll* be in this place!" said Maud Wheelspinner to Angel, "and that's a promise!"

"Are you going to go in for freak collecting someday, Angel?" said Mr. Quick in a pleasant voice. "Are you going to be like your Aunt Maud when you grow up?"

Angel's aunt answered for her as we trudged down Lake Lot, "I'm not talking about her being in this place as a collector. I'm talking about her being here as an exhibit!"

"I'm not a freak!" said Angel.

"Well, we have a lovely evening for this little adventure," said Mr. Quick. "And my son is looking forward to this visit with these monsters."

"Mon*ster*," said Angel. "There's only one."

"One human," her aunt said, "but we have some very twisted flora on the ground floor and the midges from The Moon, as well as the snakes which fell from The Star."

"I love those Stardusters myself," said Mr. Quick.

"They actually s-l-e-e-p for months, don't they?"

"They hibernate, yes."

"Fascinating! It's as though they return from the dead."

"A brilliant way to put it, Quinten! It's exactly like that!"

"Sorry to spell out the S word in front of the kids," said Mr. Quick.

"They're old enough to comprehend that the S word Elsewhere is not the same as on Alert."

"I use it all the time, anyway," said Angel.

"Because you're not a little lady," said her aunt, "you're a little abscess."

"I have never seen The Star shine brighter!" Mr. Quick enthused as he glanced up at the evening sky.

"You're a little abscess," Maud Wheelspinner continued, "and later on I may have to squeeze you to get all the pus out."

"Here we are, here we are!" Mr. Quick persisted with his jolly tone.

It was not a large building, nothing like the zoo in San Diego where my Aunt Dolly had taken me one summer. It was not a shabby tent, either, as one sideshow I had once visited was, in Coney Island, New York.

But there was a string of little lights glittering at the entrance, and a sign behind the glass was lighted, too.

It said:

WE ARE NOT OF THEM
THEY ARE NOT OF US
THE BRIDGE BETWEEN IS
LONG AND LEAN
BUT IT IS THERE.

"That's a lie," said Angel. "There isn't any
bridge."

"I think what that sign means," said Mr. Quick,
"is that there is the bridge of understanding between us and them."

"My niece knows very well what that sign
means," said Maud Wheelspinner tweaking Angel's
ear hard.

If Mr. Quick saw any of the action going on
between them he acted like someone watching a
cockroach out of the corner of his eye crawl across
the clean floor of a friend's home. He looked everywhere but at it, and even gave a little whistle, his
favorite tune, which was the commercial for his
business, played evenings before the news, on the
radio.

Flush, Flush,
Scrub, Scrub,
Off the toilet
Into the Tub!

"We'll start with the midges and snakes, and work our way up to the more exotic inhabitant," Maud Wheelspinner sang out.

"Ah, Top Freak!" said Mr. Quick. "That's what I marvel at. Everytime I see one, I thank The lucky Star for my own peppy personality!"

"You know, of course, we captured two freaks but one was snatched by your wife, for The Institute."

"I didn't know. Quinneth doesn't talk about her work with me. It's top secret, you know."

Maud Wheelspinner clapped her palm to her lips. "I made a boo boo, didn't I?" she said. "I always forget how hush hush The Institute's work is."

"No, you don't," said Angel. "You say those things deliberately! You're jealous of Mrs. Quick since she's more important than you are!"

"Certainly not richer, though," said Mr. Quick, but Maud Wheelspinner's eyes were afire with rage and I saw her fist roll to a ball and wind up.

I knew that Angel would never recover if that punch landed.

"RUNNNNNNNNN!" I hollered, and I ran, too, through the great revolving door and inside, up the stairs, taking them by twos, both of us breathless and laughing.

I lay right down on the tile floor and panted, sniffling and giggling. "Now we're both going to get it!"

Angel was standing over me. "She'll wait until I get home to give it to me. She likes being alone with your father. She says your mother doesn't appreciate him the way she does."

"Mr. Quick? Someone wants boring Mr. Quick?"

"Someone more boring wants boring Mr. Quick."

"Mr. Quick makes me t-i-r-e-d!" I said.

"My aunt makes *me* s-n-o-r-e!" she said, and she let go some zzzzzzzz's.

We laughed and laughed, the first time that had happened since I'd landed on Alert, and I wondered if I could ever be truly happy in this place, if I had to be, if Lornge ever failed me and there was no way back.

"What's the matter with you, Chester?" Angel said suddenly.

"Nothing is. I'm having fun."

"But why are you lying down? Are you all right?"

And there was the answer to whether or not I could ever be content on Alert.

I almost answered: "I'm just resting, Angel," but I caught myself, scrambled to my feet and said, "Where's this freak, anyway?"

Seventeen

We followed an arrow under a sign that said:

TOP FREAK

"Nothing else in this place compares to Top Freak," said Angel. "I don't care about what they found on The Moon, or what fell from The Star."

"How do you know those things came from The Moon and The Star?" I asked her.

"Because they s-l-e-e-p, to be crude about it. Everybody and everything *does* on The Moon and The Star and Elsewhere."

"Where besides The Moon and The Star?"

"I don't know. All that kind of information comes from The Institute, because everything Elsewhere is so disgusting."

"Have you ever heard of earth?"

"What does soil have to do with what we're talking about?"

"Never mind," I said.

"Elsewhere they have real wars, did you know that? They actually kill each other?"

"On The Moon? On The Star? Where?"

"I don't know everything, but I do know our old freak, Mr. Sandman came from there: he died. And now we have two new ones from there. One I've never even seen!"

"And the one you have seen?"

"Right this way," said Angel.

We passed through The Aquarium where there were bluegill sunfish, redbelly dace, carp and goldfish, all marked: SOMNOLENTS. I could have sworn it was a plain old Delta rice rat swimming in and out of the duckweeds in that giant tank.

"Are they all from Elsewhere, too?" I asked her.

She said, "Everything on this floor is. But if it wasn't for Top Freak, I wouldn't even come up here because I hate heights."

We were heading toward the end of Level Two.

"Where was Lornge when he was here?" I asked.

"Downstairs. That was back when Auntie was really desperate. She was taking in condemned shuteyes from The Tower of Loathing and even their lovers, those she could catch. Nothing was coming from Elsewhere. Lornge was billed as 'Tweetie's Lover.'"

"Poor Lornge."

"Don't feel sorry for him. He flew with the hummers, you know. He and Tweetie were both Radical Shuteyes."

"Lornge was?"

"Oh, yes. He would have put a bed in the street and lain down in it, if Tweetie'd told him to. He was so slowed down over that bird he was practically dead."

"That's why he didn't want to come here."

"I never saw such a slowpoke!" Angel shook her head. "When he was here, my aunt put a huge enlarged photo of Tweetie inside his cage, and he still cried out of his one eye whenever he looked at it. Sometimes love can put your brain in such slow motion you're never the same again."

"But love makes the world go round," I said, sounding as boring as Mr. Quick.

"What do you mean love makes you whirl around? I've never seen a lover do a whirl? It's too fast for slowpokes."

"I said the *world*," I told her.

"I heard you. The whirl."

I kept my mouth shut.

Soon Angel said, "Okay, we're here. Coming up: Top Freak."

We stood in front of a golden door with what looked like a huge computer built into it.

Angel reached up and pushed AutoSpeak.

"Hello? Hello? We've come to see FFE#4."

"One hello is sufficient, Angel."

She turned to me and said, "By now this thing knows my voice."

"I am not a thing, thank you, Angel. I am a very complex form of artificial intelligence. AutoSpeak. I am AutoSpeak."

Angel said, "They're all called by the same name so they don't get too big for their britches."

"We don't wear britches, Angel," it said.

"I've got Chester Dumbello with me and we're here to see Top Freak."

"Since you're under twelve, does your mother know you're here?"

"I'll be twelve in a week, AutoSpeak. And my mother is downstairs with Quinten Quick."

"Welcome then. Welcome Chester Dumbello."

"Thanks, AutoSpeak."

"While viewing FFE#4 remember not to confuse him with a shuteye. Where this man comes from, it is considered normal to s-l-e-e-p," said Auto-Speak. "Everyone s-l-e-e-p-s there."

Angel shut her eyes and stuck out her tongue, let her arms hang limply at her side and said, "Now I'll tell one."

AutoSpeak said, "That's not nice, Angel. Gower Pye can hear you."

"Gower Pye is used to me," she said.

"Gower Pye? Are you sure that's his name?"

"Mr. Pye, sure," she said. "He's FFE#4."

"Mr. Pye," said AutoSpeak, "is our fourth freak from Elsewhere."

Angel said. "I took pictures of him in his white suit to a Show and Tell one day at school, but it got the Social Studies teacher furious. She said a freak like Gower Pye should only be discussed in Health, and then only with parental permission."

AutoSpeak sounded impatient. "Mister Dumbello and Miss Wheelspinner, are you really interested in this specimen, or would you rather talk all through my introduction?"

Eighteen

Mr. Pye was living in an enormous two room cell, with an exposed toilet, BATHE & FLUSH stamped on the tank.

There was also a caged-in porch off the bedroom, where I could see him, standing in his white suit, his straw hat pushed back. He was staring up at the night sky, his back to me.

I wondered what he would do when he turned around and saw me, and I began to fear that I would end up in the empty cell beside him.

"Okay, we've seen him," I said. "Let's go."

"You're afraid of him," said Angel, "but I'm not because he's behind bars. Hey! Mr. Pye? Want a piece of candy?"

He turned around then and walked toward us.

My heart felt as though it would bang its way out of my shirt.

"I know what *you* want, don't I?" said Angel in a sugary tone that sickened me. "Him wants a tocolate bar. Want tum tocolate, Midder Pye?"

Mr. Pye just looked at us, his eyes like the eyes

of a fish on the end of a hook, unmoving, blank.

"Him loooooves tocolate," said Angel.

"He's not a baby," I said. "Why are you talking baby-talk to the poor man?"

"You don't know what he is, Chester! Maybe in Elsewhere there are no babies: maybe this is what there is, and maybe this is all there is."

She went over to a machine beside his cell and put in a coin.

I stood there unable to look my old neighbor in the eye, I was so sad for him.

I read the bronze plaque attached to his cell.

FFE#4 is from Elsewhere. It is normal for him to s-l-e-e-p. He s-l-e-e-p-s usually in the right hand room where a "bed" is. His s-l-e-e-p pattern is not typical of his species for he s-l-e-e-p-s little and usually only when it is light.

FFE#4 has a television set (though it does not transmit) to keep his environment as close to Elsewhere as possible. He does have two Elsewhere movies to view on his Video Recording Machine, and he has also for entertainment two tapes of Elsewhere music.

You may give him a treat by buying bars of Elsewhere candy from the machine.

Please don't shout at him if he is s-l-e-e-p-i-n-g.

His name is Gower Pye.

He is 54 years old.

*   *   *

Mr. Pye knew he was going to get a treat and he stood waiting by the bars.

"Do you want to feed him?" Angel asked me. "I've fed him so much it isn't a big thing to me."

She put a Butterfinger into my hand.

It had been a long time since I had seen or tasted one, all the while I pretended to have never laid eyes on the yellow wrapping or smelled the chocolate peanut scent, or felt it crunch in my mouth.

"It looks good," I said in a casual tone. "Maybe I'll try it!"

"Don't!" said Angel.

"No, Mr. Dumbello," said AutoSpeak. "Never eat food from Elsewhere. For all you know, it could affect you so that you would feel their fatigue, or worse."

"All right, all right!" I said.

"My AutoEye is always trained on FFE#4's space, Mr. Dumbello, for your information. I see everything in that area."

Angel whispered to me, "I had a crumb of one once. It tasted like our Jump Rope Bars."

I held The Butterfinger up between the cell bars and Mr. Pye took it. He shoved it into the pocket of his suit. I noticed then how dirty that left pocket was from the chocolate melting inside. I remembered how he always favored M&M's because they didn't melt.

Angel said, "Usually he goes to s-l-e-e-p after he has candy, but you can't count on it. He's very moody, if you ask me, for someone who can do whatever he likes."

"What if he likes to go for long walks by himself at night?" I said.

"He can't do that," said Angel.

"What if he wants to see another movie instead of the two he has over and over?"

"He can't do that," said Angel.

"What if he wants to go for a ride in a boat?"

"No way," said Angel.

"What if he wants to go for a ride in a boat, in the dark, and sing?" I said.

Angel shrugged, "You can't have everything."

"What if he wishes he had some candy besides Butterfingers? How would you like it if you had to eat Jump Rope bars the rest of your life?"

"He's a freak, Chester. You're giving him a real person's desires. He's happy. Look at him."

He had wandered over to the center of the living room. There was a hardback chair facing the television. There was a table with a lamp on it. There was a braided oval rug on the floor. There was an old-fashioned tape recorder.

"He has more room than I have," said Angel, "since Maud The Fraud takes up the whole upstairs. She's got two whole rooms to herself and my room is the size of a closet."

Then we heard the voice of Maud Wheelspinner.

"Your new room," she said, "will be *in* the closet."

Angel clapped her hand across her mouth, a familiar gesture of Angel's, and her face turned red with humiliation.

AutoSpeak said, "Your aunt wants you to come out of there now, Angel. She says you are to go directly to her office. She'll meet you there in a little while."

"Oh, nooooo," Angel moaned.

"Oh, yes," said AutoSpeak.

Then Mrs. Wheelspinner was back on the system. "I'm expecting you, Brat! You'd better arrive here promptly or you know what will happen!"

"Oh, noooo," Angel said.

"What will happen if you're not there promptly?" I asked.

Her little mouth was trembling and her eyebrows were furrowed with fright.

"Yes, what *will* happen?" asked AutoSpeak.

"Keep your little trap shut, my precious, or it will be a worse punishment than you have ever had!"

"Please Auntie! Don't be cruel!"

"Auntie isn't cruel, Dear. Auntie is only looking out for her little Angel," and she laughed wickedly, a witch's wicked kind of laugh.

"GET DOWN HERE NOW!" she commanded next, and beside me, Angel shivered.

"Do you want me to come with you?" I said.

She shook her head no, as her aunt said, "ON THE DOUBLE, BRAT! . . . and as for you, Chester, your father is on his way up to see Top Freak before he takes you home. So stay where you are!"

AutoSpeak said, "Go along now, Angel. Your aunt is waiting."

That was when I heard Mr. Pye whisper, "Help her, Dumbello! Rescue her! If you don't, who will?"

AutoSpeak said, "Perhaps Mr. Pye will play you one of his tapes, Chester Dumbello. He has two."

Randy Travis and Garth Brooks, I bet.

"Play Randy Travis," I said, for I knew he liked him best.

"You can hear Guns 'N Roses doing 'Appetite for Destruction,' or Anthrax doing 'Antisocial,'" said AutoSpeak.

Oh, Mr. Pye, I thought, you hate Heavy Metal!

"Or," said AutoSpeak, "why don't you show Chester Dumbello one of your movies? How about *Terminator 2*?"

I had a sudden image of Mr. Pye peacefully poling his flat-bottomed skiff through Old Muddy with only the swamp critters calling out under the stars, and the moon peeking through the banners of Spanish moss hanging from the cypress trees.

I found it hard to look into his eyes.

Then Mr. Quick appeared, snapping his Pep-Gum happily, and calling out, "Hello there, Freak! Had any good dreams lately?"

Mr. Quick bent double laughing at the notion of sleeping dreams, as everyone on Alert seemed to find the idea of them hilarious.

Mr. Pye walked out to his porch.

"Come back here you s-l-e-e-p-i-n-g freak!" Mr. Quick began to shout. "Get your tail back here so I can get a good look at you!"

AutoSpeak said gently but firmly, "Now, Mr. Quick, you know we don't allow our freaks to be abused. Go easy, Mr. Quick, or I will *have* to ask you to leave."

"Go to sleep!" Mr. Quick cursed.

"I don't have to take that, Mr. Quick," said AutoSpeak, and suddenly a metal sheet descended from the wall, hiding Mr. Pye's cage.

Across it was written:

SAY NIGHTY-NIGHT TO GOWER PYE,
BLOW A KISS, FOR IT'S GOODBYE
SIDESHOW OPEN NEXT A.M.
THANK THE STAR YOU'RE NOT LIKE THEM!

Nineteen

Y O W!
Y O W!
Y E E - O W W W W W W!

"What was *that*, Mr. Quick?"
"It sounded like an owl to me."
"Owls hoot, sir."
"Do they? I thought they went Yow!"

Y E E E E E E - O W W W W W!

"Hurry along," said Mr. Quick as we went down the stairs of the building. "That's just an owl up on the roof."
"That's not an owl, sir. That's Angel screaming."
"She has this fear of heights, you know. That's very difficult to cure."
"She's being punished, sir."
Mr. Quick laughed. "Now I'll tell one," he said.
"I should help her! I should rescue her!"
"I think Top Freak got your ear, did he?"

"No," I said, for fear I would get Mr. Pye into worse trouble than he was already in.

"That 'rescue her' stuff is straight from the mouth of Top Freak, so don't try to fool me, Chester." He paused a moment and then added, "Son."

"Why does Miss Wheelspinner hate Angel so much?" I asked.

"You know, Son, Angel likes to get attention. If you ask me, she's not at all afraid of heights. She just likes everyone to notice her . . . I suppose Top Freak told you that fib, too: that Maude doesn't like her own niece."

"No. He didn't tell me anything. He didn't have to. I have ears and eyes. Anyone can see it."

"He's a very clever fellow, Top Freak is. I talked to him one day and we had quite a conversation. It's possible to forget completely that he s-l-e-e-p-s, *and* dreams, I might add, though he said his dreams were of night horses, so he tried to s-l-e-e-p in the daytime."

"Nightmares," I said.

"Yes, that's what he said. Apparently where he comes from there are horses for the day and horses for the night. It must be a very slack place: even the horses can't go night and day."

We walked out the front door of The Sideshow and stood on the steps. In the distance, towering over all of Lake Lot, stood The Star Reacher.

Mr. Quick looked up at it as I did.

"I could certainly use a slide and a swim," he

said, "Could you?" Then he added, "Son?"

"Yes, sir," I said.

Y O W! Y O W! U M M U M M from above us, as though in the midst of Angel's cries, someone had stifled them.

"Poor Angel," I said.

"She's anything but poor," said Mr. Quick. "She and her father are heir to Maud Wheelspinner's fortune. If I were heir to such a fortune, I would be a little more considerate toward my benefactor, but nooooo, not Angel. She treats Maud like dirt."

"I would say it's the other way around."

"Maud has the money," Mr. Quick shrugged.

"Don't people who have money have to be considerate, too?"

"Not really. People will love them whether or not they're considerate. Which reminds me, Chester. I have an errand to do before we swim. I want to buy some perfume for Angel's aunt, to thank her for asking us here."

"Isn't The Sideshow open to all the public?"

"It is. But it's seldom that the Top Curator invites people personally, so I may step down the street and get her a bottle of Lively."

"Yes, sir."

"Why don't you run along and play on The Star Reacher, and I'll be there very soon," he said, and I thought giddily of the nap I could sneak in, for I was getting tired.

"Another thing, Chester."

"Yes, sir?"

I was trying to see up on the roof without his noticing it, but I could not get a good look.

"Why did AutoSpeak call you Dumbello?" he asked.

"Angel forgets that my name was changed to Quick, sir."

"But why don't you correct her? Why don't you correct AutoSpeak?"

"I don't like to correct people, or machines, I guess."

"For someone who doesn't like to correct people you do a lot of it, though, at least where Angel is concerned. We say she's not being punished and you correct us. All the time."

"Yes, sir, that's how I feel."

"I hope you're not slowing up over Angel. She's never going to get any of her aunt's money so she wouldn't be my choice for you, Chester . . . I sometimes think Lornge is a bad influence on you."

"What does Lornge have to do with it, sir?"

"Lornge has the stick-by-me's, I told you that. And when he got himself so involved with Tweetie it's very possible some of Tweetie rubbed off on him. He's a little slack himself."

"I never noticed, sir."

"ELLLLLLLLLP" from the roof.

Mr. Quick glanced upward. "Did The Moon ever look so round and golden?" he said. "Well, I'll see you later, Chester. . . . Son."

Twenty

I ran back into The Sideshow, and stood just inside the door long enough to slip off a sock, put my shoe back on, and crawl on all fours toward AutoSpeak's lens.

It had not seen me coming, and was focused straight ahead, relaxed, thinking it was alone.

Quickly I felt the lens with my fingers, to see if a sock would cover it sufficiently.

"Who's playing peek-a-boo?" said AutoSpeak. "Are you loose again, Angel?"

Then I slapped the sock across it, stood up, and rolled it down securely.

"Who is that?" AutoSpeak asked.

I headed toward the stairs, not sure if there was an elevator in the building.

As I ran up, I could hear AutoSpeak repeating "Who is that?"

By the time I was past the Third Level, and almost up the ladder to the roof, AutoSpeak was saying: "Emergency! Emergency! AutoSpeak's ocular function is out of order."

Slowly I pushed open the trapdoor, felt the cool night air, and saw Angel directly ahead, tied to a pole at the edge of the roof. Her mouth was taped.

"REPEAT! EMERGENCY! THE OCULAR FUNCTION OF AUTOSPEAK IS OUT OF ORDER!"

"What do you mean, AutoSpeak? Can't you see?" Maud Wheelspinner was right above me.

"Someone has blindfolded me, Miss Wheelspinner."

"Who?"

"If I knew who, would I not say who, Ma'am?"

"I'll be right down, AutoSpeak." Then she said to Angel, "You need some time alone to think about your naughty ways, Brat. And to think about what will happen to you next! I hope you don't mind the dark and being this close to the edge. You don't, do you, Dear?"

"MMMMuhhhh!"

"Don't try to wiggle loose or you may take the pole with you as you fall to the street, Brat."

MMMMMMMuhhhhh!"

"I hate to leave you with only that one tiny spanking, in my office, but there's more coming later. Lots more! Unless this wind blows you down, pole and all."

I closed the trapdoor and went down the ladder, waiting until Maud Wheelspinner appeared, on her way to help AutoSpeak.

I curled up into a corner, closed my eyes, and almost fell asleep, though it was only seconds before her spike heels came down the ladder rungs.

It had been a long time since I had slept. My twilight nap had been disturbed by The Sleepy People Choir and the police.

"I am coming AutoSpeak!" shouted Maud Wheelspinner.

"Be careful, Ma'am. I think someone is in the building."

"Probably one of the maids cleaning up left a rag over your lens."

"No, Ma'am. I have a feeling of another kind."

"You don't *have* any feelings, AutoSpeak!"

I scampered back up the ladder and onto the roof.

I pulled off the tape on Angel's mouth and quickly began untying the ropes.

"I will never forget you for this, Chester!" Angel was whispering, holding her finger to her lips to remind me AutoSpeak could hear.

"Neither will your aunt forget me for this," I whispered back.

"She doesn't know it's you."

"She'll do something horrible to you until you tell her."

"She'll never do anything to me again," said Angel. "I'm going to run away."

"Where can you go?"

"There's only one place to hide. South Alert."

"I'll go with you," I said.

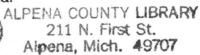

"We have to hurry. AutoSpeak will be on again and then she'll know you're in on it. I want her to think I was kidnapped."

I had the ropes off.

"But who would kidnap you, Angel?"

"Anyone could. Aunt Maud is very rich."

We ran together toward the trapdoor, while she told me, "On the Second Level there are some back stairs AutoSpeak can't see. Take the door next to Top Freak's and meet me there, but hurry!"

She went down the ladder ahead of me.

"Don't kidnap me, please!" she shouted for AutoSpeak to hear.

I hurried after her but my feet suddenly felt heavy and so did my eyelids.

I saw her reach the stairs to the Second Level.

On the last rung of the ladder, just as I was ready to run down the hall after Angel, my foot caught. I fell as I freed it, and lay sprawled on the cold marble floor.

"Why, this is someone's sock!" Maud Wheelspinner's voice . . . "Now you can see, AutoSpeak!"

I knew that AutoSpeak could not see me if I stayed on the ground, but if I stayed on the ground, Maude Wheelspinner would find me there with one sock missing.

"Whoever you are," said Maud Wheelspinner, "you don't have a chance."

I knew the truth when I heard it. My eyes closed

then, and my whole body went limp with thanks
for what was coming.

"You don't have a chance," AutoSpeak agreed
as I drifted off, and in my dream I heard a humming
growing louder and louder, and I saw the entire
Sleepy People Choir assembled on the lawn behind
my house in Lucy, Mississippi. They were singing:

> *Not a chance, lull a by,*
> *Not a chance, lool a by,*
> *Nighty, night, not a chance,*
> *Lull a byyyyyyyyyyyye!*

Twenty-one

"Is this your son?" said Inspector Clue.

"Not really," said Mr. Quick. "I could seldom call him 'Son.' I had a problem with it."

They had brought him to The Jail directly from the Wheelspinners' yard, and he was still in his wet red bathing trunks, barefoot, a towel over his shoulders.

"But he *is* your son?" Inspector Clue persisted.

"It was my wife who wanted him. Shake hands with him and see if you don't feel you have hold of a fish."

"I don't want to touch him," said Inspector Clue. "They say you can't catch it, but — "

"You can't be too careful," Mr. Quick finished the sentence for him.

They were all looking at me and wincing and smirking, the Inspector, two of his policemen, the Jailer, and Mr. Quick.

"I have to charge him," said Inspector Clue.

"You have no choice," Mr. Quick agreed. "From

the very beginning I didn't take to him. He wrote an awful poem trying to rhyme 'go' with 'door,' and when I told him they did not rhyme, he said something about a Southern accent. I should have known then."

"Do they have accents down in South Alert?" The Inspector asked, not waiting for an answer. "I know they have beds," he made a face as though he'd just taken a bite from a lemon, "but I didn't realize they spoke any differently than you and I."

"It doesn't surprise me," said a policeman. "From my own personal knowledge of these people they actually brag about being slow and slack . . . and it hasn't got a darn thing to do with love, either. I think they could easily slow their speech down to a point where door could sound like 'doe.' "

"I had a problem with calling him 'Son' all along," said Mr. Quick.

"You said that," The Inspector reminded him.

He turned to me and said, "Chester Quick I — "

"Just a minute!" Mr. Quick interrupted him. "His name is not Quick. I don't want that on record. He's Dumbello."

"That is a very peculiar name," said The Inspector.

"That's what I said. It sounded slack to me."

"A little, yes," The Inspector agreed, turning

back to me. "Chester Dumbello, you are charged with s-l-e-e-p-i-n-g in the first degree. How do you plead?"

"Guilty, but —"

"When you plead guilty you plead guilty period. There is no guilty *but*."

"Yes, sir." Maybe it was just as well, I thought, for I was ready to blurt out everything, tell them where I was from, and that I was like Mr. Pye.

But I did not want to end up in Maud Wheelspinner's Sideshow.

"I sentence you to imprisonment in The Tower of Loathing. You are to stay there until winter, and War Week, which this year will feature The Browns and The Reds in a violent squabble about how many can say 'Peggy Babcock' five times fast."

Mr. Quick said, "Peggy Babcock, Pegby Bad — that's a hard one."

"Yes. The Browns are already practicing," said The Inspector.

"Peppy Badcop — pfffft!" Mr. Quick snapped his towel with frustration.

"After that you'll be on parole for 100 days," The Inspector told me.

Mr. Quick said, "The parrot that brought him to us committed fraud, Inspector. He was on parole from The Sideshow, too. Isn't it a parole violation to bring a South Alert shuteye for adoption?"

"He might not have known Chester was a shuteye," said Inspector Clue. "How do you know he came from South Alert?"

"This boy calls him Lornge. That's probably Shuteye code," said Mr. Quick sourly. "That parrot is so twisted you wouldn't believe it. Tweetie did that to him."

"Then we'll put out an alarm for the parrot," said The Inspector.

"He cost my wife and me a lot of money!" Mr. Quick eyed me and shook his head. "We paid a handsome price for you."

"I'm sorry, sir."

"That's one thing about him," said Mr. Quick to the Inspector. "He always says 'sir' and 'ma'am.' He's got very nice manners. It's a real shame that he's so slothful."

The Inspector said, "While you're up there in The Tower of Loathing, young man, give some thought to how you want to live your life. Of course you could go back to South Alert. You'd work making exercise mats, pillows, or *worse* coffins! There's little else to do down there, unless you become a Radical Shuteye . . . and I warn you against that. With this conviction, another one for a sing-in or a s-l-e-e-p-in or any other kind of in will mean you're finished! Get it?"

"Yes, sir."

"*Then* you'll s-l-e-e-p and never awaken."

"Yes, sir."

"Do you have anything to say before the policemen take you up?"

"What if I s-l-e-e-p up in The Tower of Loathing? I don't think I can help s-l-e-e-p-i-n-g."

"We'll send a therapist to you. You can talk to the doctor about it."

"Yes, sir."

"Dr. Shrink might help you," said Mr. Quick.

The Inspector said, "You've done a lot of damage, Chester Quick. You've — "

"Dumbello," said Mr. Quick.

"Chester *Dumbello*," said Inspector Clue. "If you hadn't fallen a-s-l-e-e-p, we might have a description of the kidnapper of Angel Wheelspinner."

"I'm sorry, sir."

"Poor Maud Wheelspinner is overcome with grief," said Mr. Quick. "She sits by the phone waiting to hear what the ransom will be."

As the policemen grabbed my arms, Mr. Quick said, "Well, so long, Chester. I tried to like you. I think my wife almost succeeded in liking you but her work at The Institute always comes first."

"Winter's not that far away," said The Inspector, trying to console me, but it only reminded Mr. Quick of War Week, victorious emblems from which were sewn on to his swim trunks.

Mr. Quick murmured, "Piggy Badcop, Peggybibcop . . ."

Twenty-two

TONIGHT IN THE TOWER OF LOATHING WE HAVE INCARCERATED ONE CHESTER DUM-BELLO.

HIS SENTENCE IS FROM NOW UNTIL WAR WEEK, FOR THE LOATHSOME CRIME OF SHUT-TING HIS EYES AND S-L-E-E-P-I-N-G. HE WAS CAUGHT IN THE ACT, AND PLEADED GUILTY TO BEING A SHUTEYE!

WATCH CLOSELY AND YOU MAY SEE HIS HANDS HOLDING ONTO THE BARS OF HIS CELL. POSSIBLY YOU MIGHT EVEN CATCH A GLIMPSE OF HIS FACE.

BINOCULARS MAY BE RENTED BY THE HALF-HOUR.

IF YOU WOULD LIKE TO CALL UP TO HIM THAT YOU LOATHE HIM YOU MAY RENT A TURN ON THIS BULLHORN.

THE TOWER OF LOATHING LUNCH WAGON IS OPEN FEATURING MEATLOATHE SAND-WICHES, TOWERBURGERS, TOWERDOGS, AND TOWER TONIC!

Twenty-three

"Wake up, Chester!" said Lornge. "I've got something for you. It's Lornge."

"Lornge. Lornge. You have done me irreparable damage."

His large green eye glittered. "I have done you what?"

"Irreparable damage." I stood up and raised my arms, then bent over from the waist down and touched my toes. "You made me believe I was from someplace called The Dream Cafe, in someplace called Mississippi, on someplace called earth. I must exercise one, two, three, four, for I am *not* a shuteye five, six."

"Chester, Chester, have you been brainwashed by Dr. Shrink?"

"You have done me irreparable damage."

"Why do you keep saying that? You sound like a parrot."

"*You* are the parrot."

"You got that right. But everything else is wrong.

You really are from The Dream Cafe, and you really
are — "

"Stop!" I said. "You have done me irreparable
damage, two, three, four. Bend, and one, two, three,
four."

"Someone's done irreparable damage but it
wasn't me," said Lornge. "Snap out of it, Chester!
We don't have much time, old half a scissors!"

From the floor of my cell, I picked up the bright
gold coin, attached to the bright gold chain, held
it high and let it spin while I said, "I am not
s-l-e-e-p-y. My head does not feel heavy. My eyelids
do not feel heavy."

"No wonder! You just woke up! You've been
a-s-l-e-e-p for days!"

"I am not s-l-e-e-p-y. My head does not feel heavy.
My eyelids do not feel heavy."

From below, a renter's voice came over the
bullhorn.

"I LOATHE YOU CHESTER DUMBELLO!"

"YOU ARE A LOATHSOME SHUTEYE!"

Lornge said, "The Institute is right next door. I
have a key to your cell. You could open your door
and jump across to the roof. Then I would guide
you to South Alert where Angel is . . . Chester, why
are you staring straight ahead that way?"

"You have done me irreparable damage."

"Are you hypnotized? Is that it? Pull yourself
together, Chester! This is your chance to be free
before The Peggy Babcock Wars! Do you want to

stay locked up until winter, with people shouting up to you over the bullhorn how loathesome you are?"

I spun the coin around as Dr. Shrink had taught me, and I repeated, "I am not s-l-e-e-p-y. My head does not feel heavy. My eyelids do not feel heavy."

Lornge said, "Ah, but I'll bet you my tailfeathers you have to yawn, Chester. You have to yawn."

"You have done . . ."

"You have to yawn!"

"Me, huh huh, ahhhhhhhhh."

"Good! Right! Yawn! Yawn!"

"Ahhhhhhh roooooooooooooooo."

"Thatta boy! You're a shuteye, kid, from Lucy, Mississippi, U. S. of A., the planet earth. Don't let Dr. Shrink tell you you're not. Fight it, Chester!"

"What are you doing here?" I said as though I'd just seen him for the first time.

"I came to help you, Chester."

"Why didn't you ever tell me you were in The Sideshow? Why didn't you ever tell me you got money from the Quicks for me?"

"What do you want, my whole life history? I got you out of Lucy because you wanted to get out of Lucy. Now that's the truth as sure as my name is Lornge."

"Lornge," I said. "You have done me irreparable damage."

Part of me longed to say that I wanted badly to escape, that I was glad he had a key to the door, that I couldn't wait to see Angel! But the key word to put me under Dr. Shrink's spell was *Lornge*.

He flew down to my shoulder and nudged me with his beak.

"Chester? Fight it, kiddo, for old Lornge."

"You have done me — "

"YAWN! YAWN!"

"You   have   done   me — ahhhhhhhhhh rooooooooo."

"Do you want to get out of here?"

"You have . . ."

"Walk to the door."

"Done me, ah."

"Walk to the door! I have a key to the lock!"

"Ir-ir-ir-rep — "

"Take the key, Chester."

"Dam . . . Dam. Damage."

"Put it in the lock!"

"Okay." I was back in my own head again.

"Okay, kid?"

"Where did you get it?"

"I flew in the window while The Jailer wasn't looking . . . that's right, turn it to the left now."

The door sprang open.

We stood there in the doorway, and Lornge said, "I'll meet you over on the roof. Are you okay?"

"I am now," I said.

"Just yawn when you feel doubt, or groggy, or any of that. They've been tampering with your mind."

"Will you stay with me?"

"Yes. But now Angel needs us. They are hunting her down. Maud Wheelspinner knows she was not kidnapped, that she ran away. But she does not want anyone to think her own niece would be that unhappy at home, so she is going along with the kidnapping theory. The police are everywhere! We must be very careful. . . . Can you jump across to the roof? Can you see in this twilight?"

"I'm fine," I said, and I leapt over to the roof of The Institute.

I breathed in the fresh air, and saw in the distance The Star coming into view in the blue-black sky. I saw the Wheelspinners' grand Star Reacher looming over the Lake Lot houses.

Would I ever get back to my own house? I felt a punch of homesickness. I missed my mom, Aunt Dollar, Worms, and the old, mysterious Mr. Pye, before he was captured and put on display in The Sideshow.

Lornge was on my shoulder, and I was glad he was with me, even though everything was all his fault.

I knew blaming Lornge played into the hands of Dr. Shrink. I told myself I would concentrate on the good in Lornge, think of his sad romance with Tweetie and the faithful way he guarded over me when I took naps in the Sports Equipment Shed.

"Everything's going to be all right," said Lornge. "I'll fly down to the bottom floor, side door, and you go down in the elevator. If there are people around, take the stairs."

"All right."

"Did the therapist do awful things to you?"

"He said I must exercise hard day after day and chant that I am not a shuteye. He said that I must spin the gold coin whenever I have any doubt. He said that I must bend over from the waist down and touch my toes when I have any doubt."

"You'd better stop talking about it," said Lornge. "Your voice is getting that singsong tone to it, and I'm afraid you'll sink back into a corrective trance. Dr. Shrink tried the same thing with me when I fell in love with Tweetie. He spun the coin and made me repeat *Tweetie is not even a parrot so what am I doing with a red radish from the garden?*"

"Yes . . . but I have to warn you. Don't ever say your name aloud. Each time you do, it reinforces the brainwashing."

He said, "Lornge does? Lornge?"

Twenty-four

Somehow in my hypnotic state I headed away from the elevator and down the long corridor toward The Institute offices.

There in the largest one was Mrs. Quick in a long, white laboratory coat, holding a magnifying glass to a cage with spotlights beaming on it.

Inside, in identical white cribs, were a sleeping rodent and a sleeping pig.

"You have done me irreparable damage," I said, bending to touch my toes. "One, two, three, four."

"What is *this*?" said Mrs. Quick. "I longed to have you here and here you are. I even petitioned my father, Ivan Investigate, for permission to observe you as I do the rat here and the pig, but permission was denied because you s-l-e-p-t in public."

"You have done me irreparable damage."

"I see Dr. Shrink has been at you." She removed her latex gloves and put her magnifying glass in her coat pocket. "Listen to me," she said. "I know you can hear me through your trance. I have always known you are from Elsewhere. Both you and Mr.

Pye got here because of something I am not free
to tell you about yet."

"Irreparable."

"That shrink loves big, pessimistic words, but
he makes vegetables out of people. You can't live
a life denying what you are! I happen to think
freaks and shuteyes are the same thing, and you're
not to blame for your condition. That's why I'm on
the track of the gene that causes s-l-e-e-p. It is my
life's work!"

I raised my arms high, bent down from the waist,
and touched the floor.

"Not so much motion, please, or you'll wake up
my experiments . . . as I see my mission it is to
one day take our malfunctioning shuteyes and turn
them into productive people again. We could in-
crease our Alertian work force by ten percent,
which is the part of the population we surmise
s-l-e-e-p-s, not counting the secret s-l-e-e-p-e-r-s."

"I am not s-l-e-e-p-y. My head is not heavy."

"Listen to me. You are no good to anyone up in
The Tower of Loathing, but here you can help me
in my work. For years I have wanted to observe a
child from Elsewhere. I learn nothing from Gower
Pye, with his sticky chocolate pockets! He is
closed. He will not share with me. He will not let
me watch him s-l-e-e-p. But you. You are practically
my son, hmmmm?"

"My eyelids are not heavy."

"Here at The Institute we know there are places

in Elsewhere where people, birds, fish, insects, even plants s-l-e-e-p! But we consider it backward, a throwback to the days when man and beast were greedy and slack and stupid! We are tolerant of s-l-e-e-p when one is very diseased, and we are amused by the slowpoke behavior of lovers, but this very different s-l-e-e-p of yours is a genetic disorder, I am convinced of it!"

"My head is not heavy," I said.

"Your head is a jelly jar, if you want to know!"

"You have done me irreparable damage."

"I never told Quinten, of course. He wouldn't have taken you into the house if he'd known where you were from. I knew that Lornge would help you find places to nap."

"Irreparable."

"Will you do me a favor? Just shut up!"

!

"Sit there and keep your mouth shut."

! !   !

"I have to go home and fix Quinten his dinner. You stay here. When I return, I will find a room for you. Believe me, no one will shout up that he loathes you, either. I might even send someone down to South Alert to find a bed for you. I will treat you better than you have ever been treated anywhere but Elsewhere. But it must be a secret that you're here. I think you can understand me. I think I am reaching you through all the fog of Dr. Shrink's words. Am I? Can you give me a sign?"

All of it registered with me. I knew it was possibly my last opportunity to escape. I shut my eyes and used all my energy to summon up a yawn.

"Good! Good!"

I was back in reality.

"Don't ever say the parrot's name," I said.

She was not a dumb bird like Lornge, but Top Scientist. Her eyes became very bright. "Ah, so his name is the key word, hmmmm?"

"Yes. I slip back into the fog then. I hear you but I can't act as I want to . . . it helps some if I yawn, too."

"Okay. Now we know."

She smiled at me and I smiled back.

"Do you think you could be happy living here for a while?"

"Very. Very, very." I lied.

She removed her white laboratory coat and fluffed her hair in the mirror. "All of Alert is looking for you right now, and for your little girlfriend from next door . . . she's always been trouble, that one. Her father can build all The Star Reachers he wants, he's still stuck with a lemon for a daughter."

"She's not so bad," I said.

"How would you know?" she laughed.

"You're right, I wouldn't," I said, for I had to win her trust, or she could possibly put me in the cage with the pig or the rat while she went home for dinner.

She turned off the lights inside the cage and put

on a tape that played "The Brown March." *Brown! Brown! Brown! Brown!* the chorus sang. *Brown! Brown! Brown! Brown!*

"I love that song," I groveled. "I'm a Brown, too."

"I'm not a Brown," she said. "I'm a Red. We're all Reds here at The Institute. It's our little joke to play Brown music to keep our experiments awake!"

She opened her desk drawer and said, "How would you like a Butterfinger?"

"Very much!" I said. I could remember the crunchy feel of it, the taste of chocolate and peanuts.

She tossed it to me and I caught it with one hand.

I know Lornge was at the side door by the first floor waiting.

I said, "You have a very nice office here." I opened the wrapper of The Butterfinger. "You have very good taste."

She laughed again. "How would *you* know? Look at your clothes, wrinkled from s-l-e-e-p-i-n-g in them!" She came over to me and put out her long first finger. "And what is this in the corner of your eyes, ah?"

She flicked away the little sleep particles with a turned up lip. "Tch! Tch! Tch! All the time I've been studying s-l-e-e-p, I've never lost my revulsion at this waste you shuteyes produce there."

"I'm sorry," I said. I was beginning to fear that

I was losing ground with Top Scientist, Ex-Step-mother, so I tried, "What a lovely perfume you have on."

"I don't wear perfume. I am a scientist."

"I was honored to be your son for the short time it lasted," I said.

I was about to take a bite of The Butterfinger when she laughed and crooned, "Looooornge."

Suddenly the smell of the chocolate and the pea-nuts made me feel sick, and I put the candy bar down.

"You have done me irreparable damage," I said.

"That's the way the ball bounces," she said. "I don't trust you, Dumbello. You'd have run away if I hadn't said Lornge."

Then she sat me down in a chair, tied my hands behind my back, and wedged my mouth open with a large apple so I could not yawn.

Twenty-five

BROWN! BROWN! BROWN! BROWN!
BROWN! BROWN! BROWN! BROWN!
BROWN! BROWN! BROWN! BROWN!

I kept hearing Dr. Shrink's voice in my foggy brain, as I sat in Top Scientist's office, the Brown march hammering at my ears.

Now, Chester, it does not matter where you came from, or what the customs were there, you are HERE.

WE do not sleep.

We do not like shuteyes.

I am going to help you overcome this ugly habit by teaching you to practice exercise and denial.

Exercise and denial will get you everywhere in life.

Exercise away your s-l-e-e-p habit! That's Numero Uno!

And then: DENY THAT YOU EVER HAD IT!

BROWN! BROWN! BROWN! BROWN!
BROWN! BROWN! BROWN! BROWN!

Say "I am not a shuteye," Chester.
"I am not a shuteye, Chester!"
No! No! No! No! Don't say "I am not a shuteye,
Chester," just say, "I am not a shuteye."
Am I not a shuteye?
No! Say "I am not a shuteye."
You are not a shuteye.
No! No! No!

Although the brainwashing was evident, with
nothing said aloud I did not react.

BROWN! BROWN! BROWN! BROWN!
BROWN! BROWN! BROWN! ERRRRRRRRRRRIP!

What was that?
I listened.
The music had stopped.
Then I saw the rat running with the tape in its
mouth.
The cage door was open.
Now the pig was lumbering out onto the floor.
"MMMMMMMMRRRRRUUUUUUMM!" I said,
because I could not close my jaws.
I tapped my feet on the floor, and leaned far
forward so the pig could see the apple.
And pigs are pigs.

Twenty-six

Both the experiments ran down the corridor, in and out of offices, in a panic of freedom.

I had managed to free my hands, grab The Butterfinger from Top Scientist's desk, and chew it up as I went down the hall looking for the elevator.

When I saw the door to the staircase, where the rat and pig were cleverly hovering, I gave it a push and let them through.

I was about ready to give up on the search for the elevator, and follow after them, when I suddenly heard a sound so unbelievably sweet and unexpected that I toyed for a moment with the idea that The Butterfinger had been poisoned. Was it possible that I had died and ascended to heaven?

For listen!

BOOM! BOOM! BOOM!
What do my dreams mean, Mrs. D?
Beat on your drum and tell me.

Leeches and spiders creep into my sleep,
So does my brother and nightworms who peep,
Tell me the meaning of bullfrogs with wings,
My dreams are filled with terrible things!

I headed straight for the room from which my mother's voice, and the sound of my mother's drum, was coming.

"Mother! Mother!" I could not keep from calling out her name.

I saw her clearly sitting at a table with the drum around her neck, facing someone, no doubt doing a dream interpretation.

I shouted, "Mother! It's me! It's Chester! How did you get here? Were you looking for me?"

She did not even look up.

"Mother!" I insisted. "Are you hypnotized, too? Did Dr. Shrink tell you I was a radish and not your son or something like that?"

No answer.

A fat, curly-haired woman with her back to me leaned forward, the better to hear my mother's predictions.

I went toward them purposefully and my nose hit hard glass.

"You were right, Mrs. D, a dream of falling from a great height *does* mean that she was going down South to live," said a very deep voice.

"It could also mean she is developing foot problems, I didn't rule that out," said my mother.

I realized then that while I could see and hear her, she could not see and hear me.

No doubt I was in Top Scientist's Observation Room.

I stood by the glass partition, watching and listening, too overwhelmed with joy at seeing my mother to think of Lornge and Angel.

"No, no, no, it was definitely *not* foot problems! In such a young child? No! And now where is she but South?"

"She's South?"

"She's in South Alert, Mrs. D. She's on the lam with that perverted parrot!"

The person speaking with my mother was not a woman after all, but Angel's father, Mr. Wheelspinner, Top Manufacturer of Backyard Furniture.

"Well, maybe she is better off being there, hmmm? She is not threatened there."

"A daughter of mine in *that* evil place? I cannot bear it, I tell you! My sister predicted this would happen, that there was no way we could ever hide what she was. With every new dream I found written in her secret notebook, I knew she would be discovered."

"But she hasn't been *discovered*, Mr. Wheelspinner. She's just run off."

"Every Alertian knows no decent person would even stay overnight in South Alert, unless there was something wrong with her. That's when the shuteyes s-l-e-e-p!"

"But now she is out of your sister's way."

"And out of her will, too! That's what pains me."

"Maybe she will meet her mother, finally."

"I know you're a mother and you take a mother's side, but the woman I married is the whole reason poor Angel is a shuteye! Like mother, like daughter!"

"Top Scientist doesn't think you can inherit it."

"What does she think then when we've got two from the same house? That it's on the tables and they touched them? Is it something we're growing in our yard that gives off a virus?"

"I don't know. I'm no family counselor and I'm no scientist. What you've got going on at your place isn't my area of specialization. The dreams, I can do. The rest is your kettle of fish, Mr. Wheel-spinner."

"Some kettle of fish! My own sister says I'm a shuteye lover so what did I expect my child would be like?"

"Well, she loves freaks."

"She's a freak *collector*. There's a difference. And these freaks are from a backward place where it's allowed."

"It's not only allowed, everyone does it."

"My sister did all she could to try and keep Angel

wide-awake. But Angel is bad to the bone, I tell you, slack as they come!"

"There are worse things," said my mother.

"Sure, there are. There's death and taxes, they're worse."

"What is the news of my son? You told me you would keep me posted."

"The news is not good. I have been trying to spare you. . . . He is in The Tower of Loathing for s-l-e-e-p-i-n-g in public."

"Are you teasing me?"

"I wouldn't tease about anything that bad. How could I with a child who's a secret s-l-e-e-p-e-r? Or *was*. By now she's probably in some *bed*, in some *bedroom* down in South Alert, no longer safely curled up behind the washing machine in our basement."

"Where I come from kids do worse than sleep."

His face reddened from the obscenity. "Worse than s-l-e-e-p? What could be worse?"

"A lot could be," said my mother. "We all s-l-e-e-p where I come from."

"Now I'll tell you one, Mrs. D. You'd be in The Sideshow with Gower Pye if that was true."

"Not with my gift I wouldn't. I have a gift, and Top Scientist heard about it. She sent scouts to find out about me, and to proposition me. You can bring your son, she promised. He will have a place to live with a Star Reacher right next door. I didn't even know what that meant."

"You *didn't*? It must be intolerably backward there. Thank The lucky Star you're here."

"I wish that I wasn't now."

"You can't blame yourself for wanting a better life for you and your son . . . Now I see things more clearly. You son is from Elsewhere, too, hmmm? A freak himself."

"Here a freak, there the average."

"I like you anyway, Mrs. D. It's your own private business . . . what are you looking for in our world?"

My mother shook her head. "That was my mistake. I thought of fame and fortune, and I thought of my dear son who never went anywhere his rich Aunt Dolly didn't take him. Here would be his chance. I thought we'd be together. I had no idea Quinneth Quick would stick me in here."

"When I first went to her and told her about Angel, she said since Angel dreamed there might be an answer, but there isn't. I can see that now. You can tell me what her dreams mean, but not how to stop her s-l-e-e-p-i-n-g . . . now it's too late."

He stood up. "I wonder if I can trust Mrs. Quick to keep this quiet."

"She's tricky," my mother said.

"She's ambitious," said Mr. Wheelspinner.

"They're the same thing," said my mother. "Those types always dream of flying all by themselves . . . and they usually have sinus trouble, too."

"You have a good head on your shoulders," he said. "I would think you could whip this little problem of the s-l-e-e-p-i-n-g if you just set your mind to it."

My mother yawned.

Mr. Wheelspinner winced. "Give you people an inch, you people take a mile. You could have waited until I was gone to do something that disgusting!" he said.

Twenty-seven

"What do you mean I can't get her out?"

"You were lucky to get yourself out," said Lornge, "but your mother is Top Experiment. She is in The Room With Ten Locks. You have to leave her behind if you want to save your own skin."

"What will Mrs. Quick do to her?"

"She'll keep monitoring her, I suppose. She'll keep giving her plenty to eat and she'll keep seeing that she gets her s-l-e-e-p. And she'll keep trying to find shuteyes whose dreams your mother can interpret."

I was walking through the black night with Lornge on my shoulder, following a hidden path which he said led to South Alert.

"I don't know why I trust you," I said. "You never even told me my mother was here."

"She's the whole reason you're here. Mrs. Quick thinks she'll be able to figure out why shuteyes have to s-l-e-e-p from what your mother says about their dreams."

"If I'd only known she was here!"

"If you'd known you would have blown your cover trying to contact her or even trying to rescue her, though in the beginning she might have resisted a rescue. She liked all the attention, and everyone told her you would be getting the very best education, and that you were living with Top Scientist's family."

"How did poor Mr. Pye get mixed up in all of this?"

"I found Gower Pye myself while I was doing surveillance on The Dream Cafe. The thing about him was he liked s-l-e-e-p-i-n-g in the daytime, when most Alertian children are in school or at Playpark. Nighttime is for visits to The Sideshow. We didn't want our children to *see* him s-l-e-e-p-i-n-g . . . I took him first, one night when he was cursing his lot in life, out on one of his walks. He was for Maud Wheelspinner. I bought a burial plot for Tweetie with the money she gave me."

"What about the money you got for me from The Quicks?"

"I bought a headstone for Tweetie's grave. The big catch was your mother, though, not you. I won my parole fetching Mrs. D here."

"What I don't understand is how did someone from here ever find out about my mother?"

We send secret missions Elsewhere. We have to know what's going on Elsewhere. Otherwise, someday we would have one of your spacecrafts landing on Alert."

I shrugged. "Would that be so bad?"

"It would be the end of our civilization, and the beginning of things like wars people die in, and rooms they s-l-e-e-p in."

Then Lornge hopped up to my head and flexed his wings. "We're getting closer."

"It's so dark."

"Of course. Because most of them are a-s-l-e-e-p. It's almost midnight."

A single streetlight glowed beside a gate with a large padlock.

A sign attached to the gate said:

Ho hum, stranger, welcome to South Alert.
This is the home of Rest Forever Coffins,
Slowpoke Exercise Mats, and Proud
   Pillows.

If you are a visitor: be at ease among us!
If you are a shuteye, get your zzzzz's among us!

Lornge said, "The gate is usually open, but it's locked tonight because the police have been looking for you and for Angel's kidnapper. The police are very rowdy and the shuteyes try to keep them out from midnight until daybreak."

Lornge flew from my shoulder to the gatepost.

"Ho hum!" he called out.

"Ho hum! Who is it?"

"Lover of Tweetie," he said, remembering this time not to say his name.

"Ho hum! Who is with you?"

"A shuteye needing sanctuary," said Lornge.

"Come ahead then."

Lornge hopped back on my shoulder. "You need a new name to fool the police. We'll call you Gower Gate."

"What kind of a name is Gower Gate?"

"Gower is Mr. Pye's first name and this is a gate, isn't it?"

"I don't like that name," I said. "We have to think of another name."

The gatekeeper was a very tall, skeletal man, with a visor cap on and a pipe in his mouth.

"I have a name for you," he spoke up, smiling into my eyes and smelling of some sweet tobacco. "How about jailbird?"

Lornge hopped up and down on my shoulder. "Who are you? What is this?"

"Ho hum!" he said. "I'm Ivan Investigate. And this? This is an arrest."

I heard the fluttering sound of Lornge's wings, followed by gunshot.

Twenty-eight

THIS MORNING IN THE TOWER OF
LOATHING WE HAVE RECAPTURED CON-
VICTED SHUTEYE, CHESTER DUMBELLO.

HIS NEW SENTENCE IS FROM NOW UNTIL
WE FEEL LIKE LETTING HIM GO, WHICH YOU
CAN GUESS FROM PAST EXPERIENCE MEANS
HE WILL BE WITH US FOR QUITE A WHILE, AND
ON VIEW AT HALF TIME IN THE SPRING OLYM-
PICS ALONG WITH TOP FREAK, AND TOP
EXPERIMENT.

WATCH CLOSELY AND YOU MAY SEE HIS
HANDS HOLDING ONTO —

"Pay attention, Chester," said Dr. Shrink.
"LORNGE!"
"You have done me irreparable damage."
"Yes, he did. And what will do you good?"
"Exercise and denial."
"And so, my boy, begin!"

"Bend and touch my knees, two, three, four, I am NOT a shuteye, six, seven, eight. Bend and touch my — "

Over the bullhorn came: "YOU ARE SO LOATH-SOME I SKIPPED SCHOOL TO COME DOWN HERE AND TELL YOU YOU MAKE ME WANT TO BARF ALL OVER EVERYWHERE!"

I vaguely recognized the reedy voice of Cyril Speedway.

"Don't be distracted by the horn renters," said Dr. Shrink. "They'll be out there as long as you're in here. They think it's lucky to call up to you."

As the fog in my head thickened, I tried to think what the word "lucky" meant.

The doctor said, "People who loathe people are the luckiest people in the world."

I yawned.

"Lornge," he said, "Lornge!"

That word, too, rang a very distant bell in my memory, but it meant nothing anymore except the trigger to my mantra. "You have done me irreparable damage."

"Good! Good, Dumbello!"

Twenty-nine

Every night The Sleepy People Choir announced their approach with the eerie humming that was their trademark.

They would form a circle beneath my cell window in The Tower of Loathing, and begin with their signature song.

Lull a, lool a, lulla by

Lull a by

Loll a by

Over their own bullhorn they introduced The Tired Trio formed since I was taken into captivity, and pledged to croon to me, to keep my spirits lifted until I was freed.

When the choir was not singing, the trio was, and the music floated up to me, a balm to my spirits.

But I was fast falling apart, exhausted from the constant exercise forced on me, and from the memorization sessions, when Dr. Shrink would go over and over things with me, so that I would learn to think like an Alertian.

I would sit on the cold floor of my cell, knowing that as long as I could say something from memory, I would not be forced back on the treadmill, or made to touch my toes and do more pushups.

"My name is Chester. I don't like people who are different. I am glad I am an Alertian because we pride ourselves on being alike.

"Variety gives me anxiety.

"Variety gives me anxiety.

"Variety gives me anxiety.

"My name is Chester.

"Shuteyes are loathsome.

"Shuteyes belong in The Tower of Loathing.

"Shuteyes . . . zzzzzzz!"

"Wake up, Dumbello!" It was the jailer again, nudging me with his billy club. "You're not fooling me, Mr. Lazybones! Mr. Drowsy Butt! Get up! On your feet!"

"No one could fool *you*, sir," I groveled before him as one does before the captor, after days and days of cruelty at his hands.

"You bet your broken-down behind no one fools me! The day a s-l-e-e-p-i-n-g turd like you fools me,

I'll head down to South Alert for burial!"

He slapped my legs with his billy club. "Did you hear me? Get those lazy limbs up!"

I struggled to my feet, fell against the wall, and clung to the bars for support.

"I'm dizzy," I said.

"That's because it's a windy night, and The Tower of Loathing sways in the wind, and we're very very very high up, too, we are."

He was a disgusting-looking fellow with rotting teeth from which emerged a putrid smell like that of eggs gone bad. His grimy hands had flies on them, attracted by the grease that formed there daily as he set down my food tray, and the slop splattered on him, then hardened there, for he said he only bathed to celebrate War Week.

Below The Tired Trio shouted out in joy at the sight through their binoculars, of my knuckles on the bars.

They began to sing:

> *For he's a jolly good fellow,*
> *Our sleepy-headed Dumbello!*

The jailer said, "You don't look so hot tonight."

"I'm very dizzy."

"Don't repeat yourself! Why do you repeat yourself? Can't your sluggish mind remember what you said?"

"How long have I been here?" I asked him.

"Too long, if you ask me! Stand up straight!"

"I am," I said as I slumped down to the cell floor.

"Don't get me in trouble!" he said. "I'm going on vacation in two days up to the mountains. My whole family is coming and we're going to practice for War Week. We're all Browns."

"So am I," I managed.

"*You*? You're no color! You're the color of things expelled from the nose or the stomach or the anus. Or," and now he had himself a good laugh, "the corners of the eyes! Is it true you grow little eye-turds?"

My head hit the floor and I felt everything spin around.

"Don't croak," the jailer whispered at me nervously. "You croak and there goes the mountain vacation and the whole Guardino family winning The Peggy Babcock War for The Browns! Hey, did you die on me, Dumbello?"

"Sssssss sick," I managed.

"I'm praying to The lucky Star that's all you are! Dr. Shrink said not to give into you but he's not the one who gets canned if you pass away. I'm going over his head," he was mumbling to himself in a panicky tone, "but I have no choice. My wife has been packed for a week. Peggy Babcock. Peggy Babcock. Peggy Babcock. Peggy Badbock — oooops I need practice. I need to get away. It isn't good to be around a shuteye this long! A half-dead shuteye isn't doing the air in here any good. I think

I better get Top Scientist over here."

"Yes," I gasped.

"Yes?" he said.

I could not answer.

Over the bullhorn came an announcement from the director of The Sleepy People Choir.

"And now, just for you, Chester, a South Alert love song!"

The jailer said, "Those s-l-e-e-p-i-n-g freaks! They should be ashamed of themselves! If I didn't have to run next door to the doctor, I would throw excrement down on their heads because they're asking for it!"

He left me on the floor of my cell, eyes shut, ears soothed by soft voices singing:

I am swept away by you,
My life was slept away till you,
The world suddenly seems,
Like one from my dreams,

I had never been so tired in all my life.

I'm not only feeling slooooooow,
I'm feeling I'm about to goooooo
To sleep sleep sleep sleep sleep
Sleep sleep sleep sleep sleep sleep
Sleep sleep sleep sleep sleep sleeeeeeeeeeeeeeee!

Thirty

The sun was in my eyes.

"Finally!" a woman's voice said. "You slept for thirteen hours! Thirteen hours!"

"Good morning, Mrs. Quick."

She was wearing her long white laboratory coat, sitting on a stool, peering down at me.

"Didn't I tell you to take me up on my offer? If you were living in a room at The Institute now, you wouldn't be passed out on the floor. You'd have a bed. I was making arrangements for one the night you barged in on me in that trance. I thought we had a deal."

I sat up. "Why didn't you tell me my mother was on Alert?"

"I'm not Top Scientist because I care about little boys wanting their mothers!"

"I want to see her," I said. "I want to talk to her."

"So does she want to see you, so does she want to talk to you. If wishes were horses, beggars would ride. Do they have that expression Elsewhere?"

"How do I know?" I said. "I only know my mother says if you dream of a horse someone you know is going far away."

"Someone you know *is*," said Top Scientist. "Your jailer is off to the mountains ahead of schedule because you're giving everyone a nervous breakdown. Day and night we've got the shuteyes coming up from their ghetto to protest. Doctor Shrink's treatment isn't working on you. And now your mother is refusing to cooperate unless I break a rule."

"Am I going to see her?" I got up off the floor. "When?"

"You can't see her until you're out of here. That big a rule I can't break."

"When will I be out of here?"

"I have to go before the court and agree to be responsible for you. Then, maybe, sometime after War Week you can be transferred to The Institute."

"I'll get sick and die before then. They make me get on the treadmill three times a day. I am dizzy enough from no sleep and this swaying tower — "

"And it's very very high up, I know. I get dizzy myself coming up here . . . but hush! I have been able to get some changes through, and as I said, I am also breaking a little rule."

From down below I heard the voice of the day's first horn renter.

"CAN YOU HEAR ME, DUMBELLO? I AM NOT LIKE YOU, THANK THE LUCKY STAR! I WOULD

RATHER LIVE MY LIFE INSIDE A WORM THAN LIVE YOUR LIFE!"

"That's Cyril Speedway again," I said.

"Poor Cyril," said Mrs. Quick. "His father thinks he's a secret shuteye just because he likes to lie down and look up at the stars. He wants to be an astronomer."

"Is his father making him shout at me?"

"It's his own idea, ever since Angel Wheelspinner went off to live with the shuteyes."

"Then people know she wasn't kidnapped?"

"They say she's been seen in South Alert three or four times, always with shuteyes." Top Scientist glanced at her watch and stood up. "I have to get back, but you'll be all right now. No more forced exercise. You can s-l-e-e-p all you want. You may step out on the roof for fresh air and a change of scenery, as long as a guard watches over you. And — " She smiled suddenly and picked up a bag from the floor. "In here is a secret surprise. I'm breaking the rules, but I promised your mother you would get this, in return for her evaluation of dreams from South Alert volunteers."

I took the package from her. There was a familiar aroma. I sniffed it.

"Yes," said Mrs. Quick. "You're going to like what's in there, Dumbello."

"My mother's Dream Cake," I said, tearing at the string.

"And there's more where that came from if you

just cooperate with me. Forget trying to escape. You can't."

"Is it because Lornge is dead?" I said.

"Is it because who is dead?" she said.

"Lornge," I said. I had the fluffy yellow cake with the white frosting in my palm, headed toward my mouth, when I suddenly felt like gagging.

Top Scientist said, "Well, that much of Dr. Shrink's treatment works. At least we can control you."

"You have done me irreparable harm," I said.

Thirty-one

When my head was clear again I was alone.

I could tell it was late afternoon by the sound of the schoolchildren heading off to PlayPark.

I was happy to see The Dream Cake untouched on the table. Anything from Elsewhere was nauseating to anything from Alert so not even the Alertian flies, roaches or ants went for it.

I grabbed an enormous hunk of the cake and bit into it, tasting something familiar and wonderful. At the same time, as I chewed away my teeth hit an unexpected surprise. Paper.

My mother had managed to bake a note inside the cake.

It said:

IF YOU DREAM OF A DOUGHNUT, YOU'LL LAND ON A ROOF, IF YOU DREAM OF ITS HOLE, THE WHOLE THING'S A SPOOF. BE READY TO DREAM ONE WAY OR THE OTHER, THE DOOR ON FLOOR TWO WITH TEN KEYS LEADS TO MOTHER.

Thirty-two

"DUMBELLO?" the new jailer's voice came over the bullhorn, "THE HELICOPTER SERVING HOPELESS OFFENDERS WILL PASS YOUR CELL IN SIX MINUTES. IF YOU WOULD LIKE MILK AND DOUGHNUTS PASSED IN TO YOU, TIE YOUR SHIRT TO THE BARS."

I had it off in a second and in another it was flapping in the wind.

A new voice was on the bullhorn now. "YOUNG DUMBELLO, WE ARE YOUR FRIENDS FROM THE CHAPEL OF EBBING HOPE. WE PRAY FOR ALL LOST CAUSES — YOU'D BE SURPRISED. WHEN WE PRAY FOR YOU WE PRAY TO THE SAINT OF EYES WIDE OPEN. SEND YOUR PRAYERS TO HIM, TOO, FOR HE HAS BEEN KNOWN TO MAKE MIRACLES HAPPEN BY HEALING SHUTEYES.

"REMEMBER, TOO, THE SAINT OF EYES WIDE OPEN ENJOYS RECEIVING GIFTS OF MONEY AND IS 100 TIMES MORE LIKELY TO

GRANT A MIRACLE WHEN HE IS SURPRISED
BY WHATEVER YOU CAN AFFORD TO GIVE.
PLEASE NOTHING UNDER FIVE DOLLARS."

There was a strong breeze making The Tower
sway that night, and at the approach of the helicopter, my shirt was sucked away by the wind from
the motors.

At the same time, a buzzer sounded and the
barred window swung open. A young man jumped
into my cell and shouted, "Hurry! Get into The
Helicopter Serving Hopeless Offenders! You only
have two minutes to make your escape!"

Even with all the noise from the motors, the
voice sounded vaguely familiar, though the white
face with the frightened-looking eyes did not look
like anyone I knew.

"Did you hear me, Chester?"

I saw goosebumps up and down his arms and
his teeth were chattering. As The Tower swayed
in the wind he moaned as though he were being
tortured.

"*Angel*?" I said.

"Will you *hurry*?"

"Did you cut all your hair off?"

The blonde mop was gone. Her hair was short
like a boy's.

"I'm a Radical Shuteye now, Chester. I don't
want to look like the enemy anymore."

"But you just look like any boy, Angel."

"Yes, but I'm a girl who looks like a boy and that's radical."

"What are you doing here when you are so afraid of heights?"

"Getting you out, Chester. This isn't your struggle."

I looked down at the distant ground, and out at my shirt flying west in the wind, past the spinning blades of the helicopter. "If it's not my struggle whose struggle is it?"

"It is a struggle for shuteyes, not for aliens from Elsewhere. I wear my zzzzzzzz's proudly now, Chester. But you've got to go back where you came from!"

"But what will happen to you?"

"I'll sleep here tonight, giving you a chance to escape, and tomorrow before breakfast Friends from The Chapel of Ebbing Hope will call you down for prayers. I gave a donation to them. Of course when they call you down they'll get me. I'll get out then. Hurry!"

I crawled out onto the ledge and into the helicopter as Angel said, "Does this place always sway a lot?"

"Angel, Angel," I said, "with your fear of heights you won't be able to stand it."

"Once you saved me when my aunt had me tied to a pole on the roof of The Sideshow. Now it's my turn to rescue you. I'll tell you something: The

Friends from The Chapel of Ebbing Hope aren't cheap."

She waved at me as we pulled away and the pilot for The Helicopter Serving Hopeless Offenders said, "I should charge, too. This is a risk I'm taking."

"I don't have money."

"Tell Top Experiment she owes me big!"

Angel was waving at me and I was waving back, then clapping my arms around my bare back and chest, chilled by the night air.

"Put this on," the pilot said, handing me a blue sweater.

"Thanks."

"I dream a lot of my teeth falling out. Tell your mother."

"You're a shuteye?"

"They aren't waking dreams," he admitted. But hastily, he added, "I'm not a radical one. I live a respectable life, s-l-e-e-p-i-n-g in secret. No one knows but my wife . . . in my dreams my teeth fall out into my hand."

"That could be molar trouble," I said.

"I don't want some twit kid interpreting my dream. I'm talking about trading services here. This ride for an interpretation of my dream by Top Experiment."

"How did you know about my mother?"

"Sometimes I transport offenders to South Alert after their prison sentences. I buy their newspaper when I'm down that way, The South Alert Z-Sheet.

Your mother's famous down there. They're going to name a side street after her."

"I'll tell her your dream," I said, "but how can she let you know what it means?"

"Through the parrot," he said as we approached the rooftop of The Institute. "The parrot sends his love to you."

My heart jumped, but I didn't say Lornge's name. Not aloud, anyway.

With The Star shining bright above me, I gave it a little salute, feeling suddenly lucky. Lornge was okay!

Thirty-three

When I got to the second floor, it took me a while to find my mother's cell, which seemed inside like a living room, complete with rugs, chairs, a table and a desk, with what looked like a sleeping bag rolled up in the corner. It was really an exercise mat.

Ten keys were on a ring, under a WELCOME door-mat outside the cell.

"Hurry, Son!" said my mother. "Quinneth Quick always comes back after dinner for a last check."

She was unrolling the bag and stuffing it with a pillow to make it look as though she were inside.

"I'm still working on lock number four!" I said.

"While you're doing that let me tell you how to rid yourself of the hypnotic word so you can say the parrot's name."

"Why are all these keys so hard to turn?"

"They don't want me loose is why. They have never heard or seen such a gifted dream inter-preter. And down in South Alert, Son, they're nam-ing the main street after me."

"The helicopter pilot said it was a side street."

"A side street, a main street — what's the difference, anyway? Are you two jealous of me?"

"I'm starting on number five now, Mother."

"You will not go into the hypnotic fog if immediately after hearing *Lornge* you say: *If you mess with my head, you'll be better off dead.* Then you say, 'Only kidding.'"

"Why say only kidding?"

"To be on the safe side. You always want to be on the safe side when you make a threat."

"Then what good is the threat?"

"Threats are good to give you time to run."

"Lornge," I said, and then quickly I said, *"If you mes with my head, you'll be better off dead."*

I was doing fine. No fog. No compulsory words about irreparable damage spilling out of my mouth. I sprung the fifth lock and went on to the sixth.

"Finish saying what I said to say!" my mother said.

"Only kidding," I said.

"Never believe a threat will always work, my son. That is the road to black eyes, ugly red bruises, swollen lips, and cauliflower ears."

"Six!" I said happily, moving on to the seventh lock.

"Six is a magical number here," said my mother. "The world was created in six days."

"What happened to Sunday?"

"That's our myth. In Alert, the Lord didn't rest, of course . . . Chester?"

"Seven!" I said. "What?"

"I've been offered a lot of money to stay here. Top Scientist knows she can't keep me by force forever. You could go home and live with your Aunt Dollar."

"And leave you behind?"

My mother shrugged.

"I couldn't leave you here," I said. "You wouldn't want to stay here, would you?"

"It's the only way you'd ever get a chance to live somewhere there is a piano and napkin rings, a silver Aero Commander, and a swimming pool."

"Don't forget the friendly collie, the pony named Sailor after my father, and the Suzuki GSXR-750 racing bike," I said. I was on number eight.

"If I come home with you, Son," said my mother, "you can't go live with Aunt Dollar and Uncle Tux because it would humiliate me. People would ask why couldn't your own son stand you?"

"Nine. I'm on nine."

"Here I'd get money. I'd be very rich . . . and later," my mother's tone became soft and sad, "when they're through experimenting with me, I guess I'd take Mr. Pye's place. The rumor is he's gone."

Just after my mother said that, and as I was turning the tenth key in the tenth lock, we heard Lornge's voice.

"Mr. Pye *is* gone."

"Lornge!" I cried out. Then I said, "If you mess with my head, you'll be better off dead . . . only kidding."

Lornge had lighted on my left shoulder, and he pecked my cheek tenderly with his beak. "I don't mess with people's minds anymore. I thought you would be like Tweetie and bond with me, that we would be like a pair of scissors, but you don't have the stick-by-me's. I made the mistake of thinking because you're a shuteye, you'd understand the loneliness of life."

"I'm not a parrot, though, Lornge," I said, forgetting not to say his name. "If you mess with my head, you'll be better off dead. Only kidding."

Lornge hopped about my shoulders nervously. "Somebody's already messed with your head, kiddo. You don't sound so good."

"I can't help it," I said.

"*I* can't help having the stick-by-me's. What does it matter that you're not a parrot and I am?"

"I could maybe get the stick-by-me's but it has to be with someone more like me."

"Someone who doesn't know you can bond with anyone or anything and it doesn't matter if you're alike. What matters is what you feel together. Love is what matters."

"Ten!" I said.

The Door With Ten Locks sprang open, and my

mother came out shaking her head with an I *knew* it! rhythm.

"Free! Just in time, too, eh, Lornge? Because now there is no Top Freak, hmmm? Wasn't it you who said nothing bad would happen here? What happened to Mr. Pye? And who would be put in his place if I was still locked up? It would be me next, wouldn't it?" She had ahold of Lornge's long white tail feather, "Wouldn't it, Lornge?"

"If you mess with my head," I said, "you'll be better off dead . . . only kidding."

Lornge said, "You sound like a parrot to me."

Thirty-four

But Mr. Pye was safe and standing outside The Institute wearing a white nightdress over his soiled white suit, carrying his straw hat.

I had put on the white nightdress handed to me by a member of The South Alert Nightdress Brigade. My mother, too, wore one. And even Lornge had on a tiny bird nightdress complete with a little white nightcap, a white pom-pom at the end.

My mother beat her drum as we marched away from The Institute, all of us disguised as part of The Parade of the Nightdress Brigade.

BOOM! BOOM! BOOM! alternated with the loud snoring sounds the brigade was known for.

BOOM! BOOM! BOOM!
ZZZZZ ZZZZZ ZZZZZZ
BOOM BOOM BOOM
ZZZZZZ ZZZZZZ ZZZZZZ

"Anyway," said Lornge, "Tweetie was more fun

than you are, Chester. She knew more 'You Tell 'Ems' than anyone anywhere including Elsewhere."

"What are 'You tell 'ems'?"

"You tell 'em, Goldfish. You've been around the globe. You tell 'em, Pieface. You've got the crust."

He wasn't even laughing at Tweetie's jokes, but staring at me with his soulful eye, while the drum and the snoring sounded around us.

"Are you going to help us get back home?" I asked him.

"It's bad luck to say so before it happens," he said.

"I'm glad Mr. Pye got away, too."

He was strolling ahead of us, off in his own little world as usual, though I caught a strain or two of the song he was singing. "I've Got Friends in Low Places."

"You won't even miss me," said Lornge. "After Tweetie died I fell into all sorts of abnormalities, like repetitive behavior in which my head would weave back and forth, or I'd shift constantly from one foot to the other, pluck out all my feathers, and say nothing over and over but 'Life Is A Terrible Trap.' "

I said, "I probably won't do any of that. But I *am* worried about Angel."

"She'll be fine. Those Radical Shuteyes are like a big family. They even took *me* in at one time,

s-l-e-p-t right in front of me, too, and acted as normal as anyone. We'd sit around the table down in
South Alert and talk about War Week or sports or
gardening. I had to remind myself they were shuteyes. No offense intended."

"I wish I could see her safely out of The Tower.
And I wish I could be sure she'll like it in South
Alert. Won't she miss her father? Won't she miss
having a Star Reacher in her yard?"

"She hated that contraption. It was you who
liked that thing. That's what I mean about
you, Chester: you don't take enough notice of
people!"

"Maybe my head doesn't weave back and forth,
and I don't shift from one foot to the other, but
I'm really worried about Angel! I don't know how
she'll get through this night in The Tower of
Loathing," I said.

"Soon it'll be just a bitter memory. She's already been outfitted for a sandwich board saying
I s-l-e-e-p in the open on one side and
ZZZZZZZZZZZ is a beautiful sound on the other.
Her father doesn't want anything to do with her
for fear he'll be cut out of his sister's will . . . and
you're forgetting something, Chester."

"What?"

We were coming to a field which looked familiar
to me. Behind us there was the sound of a voice
calling "Hot dogs! Popcorn!" Then the whump of
a bat hitting a ball, and crowds cheering.

"You're forgetting that Angel's mother is in South Alert. They've had this big reunion."

I saw that the parade had stopped, and now The Nightdress Brigade was drifting away from the rest of us.

"Where are they going?" I asked Lornge.

"They're staging a s-l-e-e-p-in at The Stadium. The South Alert Shuteyes want to play The Browns and The Reds, but no one wants to play with them."

Suddenly, looking up, I saw the same long line of stars I had seen when I first landed on Alert. They reached down like fingers about to lift me off the ground.

"Are you coming with us?" I asked Lornge.

"I wouldn't be happy Elsewhere," he said. "Who would be mine there, ready to fly with me day and night?"

There was a tear in his one, big, lime-colored eye and he hopped up a little away from me, turning the blind eye toward me.

"We've been through something together that I'll never forget," I told him. "When you go through something with someone, you remember."

Then I heard Mr. Pye's voice ahead of us, protesting, "Wait a minute! What the — ?"

And suddenly my arms were spread the same as a bird's wings, and behind me my mother said, "I forgot my drum!"

"You'll get another, Mother," I called over to her,

as I watched her follow Mr. Pye up into the night.

I moved my arms and my feet left the ground where the tear from Lornge's eye shined in the moonlight.

"I'll miss you," I called to him. "Goodbye! I'll be thinking of you!"

He gave a cluck and said, " 'You tell 'em, parcel post. I can't express it.' "

Thirty-five

"Good evening, ladies and gentlemen, This is *30 Minutes*, and tonight we are bringing you an exclusive interview with Rita Box-Bender, only friend of Chester Dumbello, the boy who visited Planet Alert with his mother."

There was Worms standing in front of her house, by the card table with the coffee cans on it, filled with angleworms, spot tail minnows, and dead flies.

My mother fanned herself with a page from her new book contract and said, "Remember when she was this pasty-faced poor thing out there living with the moonshiner? Now she's on the TV thanks to us!"

"Shhhhh," I said. "I want to hear this."

Worms had on face makeup, lipstick and eyeliner. She was looking right into the camera's eye telling how Planet Alert was a mysterious place where the people were blue and the sky was red.

"And how big are the people, did he tell you that?"

"She did. She said they're little. The adults are no taller than water fountains and the children are the size of fire hydrants."

I groaned and gave my mother a look. "Why didn't you just tell her the truth?"

She waved the book contract at me. "People don't want the truth. People want flying discs that give off orange glows, and little green men with domed heads and insect eyes."

"We don't even know that Alert's a planet," I said.

"We don't even know if we're one. The truth has a way of changing. My great-great-grandfather would have bet the land he lived on nothing could fly but birds. He died not knowing the word 'airplane.' "

My mother was not allowed to be interviewed by anyone, anymore, and neither was I, or she would have to return the money the publisher had already paid her to write her book.

The title was to be

GRABBING THE DREAM

A Story of the Abduction by Extraterrestrials of Madame Dumbello, America's Foremost Dream Interpreter.

Worms was saying, "On Planet Alert it's not normal to sleep."

Ha! Ha! Ha! from the interviewer. "I think that's a little far-fetched, Ms. Box-Bender. Was your best friend pulling your leg?"

"He said if you were caught sleeping in public you were sent to prison."

"Now I'll tell one," said the interviewer jovially. "What's that there on the card table?"

My mother said, "See that, Chester? The truth doesn't keep the cameras rolling."

"This is the bait table," said Worms, "but I also have my tinfoil ball under it which is too heavy for me to lift. I've been saving tinfoil all my life, since we save everything: paper, string, orange seeds, grapefruit rinds, and bureau drawer handles."

"How much did these little blue guys on Planet Alert weigh, did either of the Dumbellos tell you that?"

"No. And I have some of my soap bars here, too, which I made from bacon grease and lye. I've been homeschooled since I was ten years old."

"Getting back to the Dumbellos, how would you describe Mrs. D, Chester's mother?"

"Now she thinks she's important so her dream interpretations cost more."

My mother said, "Now she *knows* she's important so her dream interpretations cost more. And *you*, Worms Box-Bender are only appearing on the boob tube because of her importance!"

The interviewer was broadcasting from Atlanta, Georgia, on a split screen with Worms. He said, "Ms. Box-Bender, you said you'd written a poem about the Dumbellos' trip to this faraway planet."

Worms said, "I didn't write it. Edgar Guest did. I just memorized it."

The show closed with her reciting it.

The Things that Haven't Been Done Before,
Those are the things to try,
Columbus dreamed of an unknown shore,
At the rim of the far-flung sky.

One day my Aunt Dollar drove up in her big, white Rolls Royce. Everybody'd come running, calling out things like "Hey, Dumbell, there's an extraterrestrial millionairess wants to chauffeur you to Planet R U NUTS! Come on out! It's against the law to sleep, remember!"

Aunt Dollar said, "I'd like to take you back to Mobile with me for a while, nephew, but if you come with me, don't say a single word about this scam your mother's cooked up to defraud the public."

She should have known me well enough by then to know I never would.

"But it really happened," I told her.

"And I'm The Queen of The Cotton Bowl. . . . Just zip up your lips, Chester, for very rich people like your Uncle Tux and I don't find that sort of thing amusing, as the rabble seem to. I've never heard of an extraterrestrial appearing to a millionaire, a corporation head, a United States senator, or a bank president."

"Maybe they're all too busy," I said.

"Or too realistic," said Aunt Dollar.

"On Alert, they have these slides called Star Reachers," I said. "You can whip down one like you're on a roller coaster ride and end up in the pool."

"Maybe you better just stay in Lucy."

"I was planning to, anyway."

"That Unidentified Flying Object/ E.T. type talk attracts crazies: people who carry all their belongings around in boxes and sleep in city parks. Your Uncle Tux says every one of them is looking for a handout."

"Well, I'm not. And my mother's not, either."

We had to turn people away from The Dream Cafe most days. My mother had so many customers she'd work way past dark. Lornge's old cage became her bank, and by day's end, it'd be jammed with five and ten dollar bills.

There were times I'd hear him telling me we were like scissors, or complaining that I didn't have the stick-by-me's.

(You tell 'em, Pieface. You've got the crust!)

Some nights when the birdcage was filled with money, and my mother was sitting down at her word processor to do another chapter in her book, I'd tell her I was going for a walk.

"I hope you're not worrying about everyone on Alert, the way you take these walks of yours."

"It isn't that," I said.

It wasn't, either. All of it seemed so long ago I hardly remembered what Lornge looked like. His name had no effect on me any longer. I barely remembered what it was I'd begun spouting off at the sound of it.

But sometimes I'd get a restlessness that wouldn't let me just sit like a stick in front of the TV, or lay on my stomach up in my room reading. I'd have to go. And going, I would think about things. I'd wonder if Angel ever survived that night in the swaying Tower of Loathing. And if she had, where was she now? Was she living in South Alert with her mother, coming up nights humming with The Sleepy People, or marching in The Nightdress Parade, wearing her zzzzzz's?

Or was she back living on Lake Lot, still teasing Cyril Speedway in school, sleeping behind the automatic washer in the cellar, and being tortured by Maud Wheelspinner?

I never heard about a missing person that I didn't wonder if he or she was captured for The Sideshow? Who was the new Top Freak, and was it another loner like Mr. Pye? That's what my mother called him.

She'd say, "Did I tell you he doesn't want to be written about in my book? Says to me just pretend he wasn't there."

"He's shy, maybe."

"Shy? *Him?* No. He just doesn't have any stalls

in his stable, if you know what I mean, Son. Anybody in his right mind would give anything to have his name in a book, maybe be interviewed the same as Worms, in front of the whole country on a Sunday night!"

"Maybe he doesn't want the attention," I said.

"He never did. I wonder how someone gets that way? You know what I mean? What does it take to turn a little boy into a man as strange as Gower Pye?"

"I don't know."

"Something must have happened to him. Something major."

I'd think about that, too, on my walks, and I'd wonder if something major had to happen, or if it just turned out sometimes someone was different than the rest.

And now and then I'd try saying Peggy Babcock five times fast, but I wasn't good at it, and never would know who was the best War Week, The Browns or The Reds?

I'd head down toward Old Muddy, phantom gnats flying by me in great swarms, mosquitos whining and diving by me, the crickets cheeping and the bullfrogs going jug-a-rum, jug-a-rum.

My footsteps on the spongy earth would make all kinds of life stir and call out and plunge in, the Spanish moss curtaining down from the cypress trees, the smell of swamp harsh and familiar . . .

far, far off there were ship noises, and nearer the *fwosh, fwosh* of the flat-bottomed skiff heading in from the fish hole.

The black, black water'd look like silk in the bright moonlight as he'd pole up to a bank, toss out his looped rope to the tree stump, his white suit gleaming in the feathery foliage, matching the white water lilies.

He'd jump across, carrying his catch, some goggle-eyed perch and some jack-fish.

Other things would jump, too, off the bank and into the darkness, heading down toward the muddy bottom.

"Hello!" I'd call out.

He'd give me a slight salute, or he'd be brushing the bugs away, I was never certain which.

A while ago I would have asked him all the questions on my mind. Asked him what he thought of Alert and how come he never said a thing about it. Asked him if he'd hated being Top Freak, and if he'd felt discouraged, and was he glad Lornge had come finally and rescued him?

A while ago I would have come upon him only by accident, or to view him as an oddity, and he would sense that. He would tell me anything he had to say in this cross tone, staring off in the distance where he wished I was, or he was, one of us was.

These days he'd grunt, and maybe say, "You here again?"

I'd take a page from his book and not answer him.

We'd go along.

Once I'd told him that I saw a red-bellied pond slider sink his teeth into a salamander and he'd said, "Turtles don't have teeth. They're the only reptiles that don't."

But mostly I was content not to say a thing to him. I believe he knew I wouldn't, for he didn't try to walk faster than I could as we'd head home side by side from Old Muddy.

THE END

Our revels now are ended. These our actors,
As I foretold you, were all spirits, and
Are melted into air. . . . We are such stuff
As dreams are made on, and our little life
Is rounded with a sleep.
            The Tempest — William Shakespeare